"What was it, A[...] reason we don't [...]"

"Look. I don't mean to be... It's just...complicated."

"So I gathered," Maria said under her breath. She slipped into her running shoes. Movement still hurt but it felt good to be going outside.

Her hand was on the door handle, ready to go, when Austin placed his hand on the door. His gaze was intense. He looked tormented and...hungry. Before Maria knew what had hit her, her back was against the door and Austin pressed his lips to hers. Her body ached to be touched by her husband. Her hands splayed out on his chest and she could feel his rapid breathing through her fingertips. Her fingers flexed along the smooth lines of his muscled chest.

Austin pulled back way too fast. "That was a mistake."

"Really, Austin? Was it? You kissed your wife. I don't think anyone's going to arrest you for doing what every married couple across the nation does," she whispered.

"I don't want to take advantage of the fact that you can't remember and the doctor says that I can't bring you up-to-date. It would be so much easier if I could," he said. "But you'd feel different about me, about *this*." He kissed Maria again and her knees almost buckled...

TEXAS SHOWDOWN

USA TODAY Bestselling Author

BARB HAN

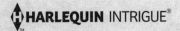

Many thanks to Allison Lyons, who is a dream editor! Also, my thanks to Jill
Marsal, who is the best agent! It's my great fortune to work with both of you.

Brandon, Jacob and Tori, the three of you inspire me in so many ways every
day. I love each of you so much and appreciate all of the adventures we share!

Babe, how lucky are we to get to spend every day with so much love and
laughter! You're the best person I could hope to be on this adventure with
and I love you with all my heart.

ISBN-13: 978-1-335-72128-0

Texas Showdown

Copyright © 2017 by Barb Han

Recycling programs
for this product may
not exist in your area.

Printed in U.S.A.

HARLEQUIN®
™ www.Harlequin.com

USA TODAY bestselling author **Barb Han** lives in north Texas with her very own hero-worthy husband, three beautiful children, a spunky golden retriever/standard poodle mix and too many books in her to-read pile. In her downtime, she plays video games and spends much of her time on or around a basketball court. She loves interacting with readers and is grateful for their support. You can reach her at barbhan.com.

Books by Barb Han

Harlequin Intrigue

Cattlemen Crime Club

Stockyard Snatching
Delivering Justice
One Tough Texan
Texas-Sized Trouble
Texas Witness
Texas Showdown

Mason Ridge

Texas Prey
Texas Takedown
Texas Hunt
Texan's Baby

The Campbells of Creek Bend

Witness Protection
Gut Instinct
Hard Target

Rancher Rescue

Harlequin Intrigue Noir

Atomic Beauty

Visit the Author Profile page at Harlequin.com.

CAST OF CHARACTERS

Maria Belasco—This FBI agent took a hit that scrambled her brain. Will she remember who put her in the hospital before he comes back to put her in the morgue?

Austin O'Brien—The second-oldest O'Brien's nickname is Ivy League. All the logic in the world can't seem to bring him to sign the divorce papers sitting on his desk. But can he risk his heart a second time around when Maria's life is on the line?

Tommy Johnson—The sheriff who grew up at the O'Brien ranch and considers them family.

Special Agent Mitch DeCarlo—How far will he go to win Maria back?

Maintenance Man Dave—Was he careless with his keys or does he know more than he's letting on?

Garrett Halpern—How much does this ex-cop know?

Tyson Greer—How involved is this neighbor?

Special Agent Cliff Ford—Could he be involved or is he on the up-and-up?

Special Agent Wheeler—He's taken over Maria's caseload. Is he missing something that can crack her case wide open?

Ansel Sanders—How far will this suspect go to silence Maria?

Aunt Bea—Has she been hiding information about the deaths of her brother and sister-in-law?

Uncle Ezra—Does he know more about the deaths of his brother and sister-in-law than he's letting on?

Chapter One

"You didn't have to take a bullet to get me to stop by and see you," Austin O'Brien teased Sheriff Tommy Johnson as he entered room 119 at Bluff General Hospital. Tommy was more like family and had grown up on the ranch alongside all six O'Brien sons. At six feet tall with light brown hair and eyes that matched, he looked like he could be an O'Brien.

"If I'd known that's all it would take, I'd have done it years ago," Tommy retorted. He'd been shot in the line of duty a few days ago. A two-hour surgery later to remove a bullet fragment from a rib and he'd been recovering nicely. At least his sense of humor was returning. That was a good sign. The first day he'd been too full of morphine to crack a smile and no one had felt like joking.

Between Austin and his five brothers, one of the O'Briens had been at Tommy's bedside since the incident. They'd been taking turns stopping by, making sure he had everything he could ever want.

"I figured you'd be tired of trying to choke down

hospital food by now." Austin opened the container of homemade spaghetti, set it on the tray table next to the bed, and positioned the stand where Tommy could access it. "Just don't rat me out to the nurses."

"Janis made this?" Tommy asked with a smile. She'd been employed at the ranch for more years than Austin cared to count. So much so, she was more family than employee and the boys had voted to give her shares of the family ranch and Cattlemen's Crime Club now that they'd inherited the place.

"You know it," Austin said, taking a step back and crossing his arms as Tommy picked up the fork and dug in.

"I forgot how good a cook she is," he said after swallowing the first bite.

"Stop by for Sunday supper anytime. Or any other night of the week, for that matter." Austin took off his white Stetson and set his hat on the foot of the bed. Tommy already knew about Sunday meals being a big deal and they'd become even more important recently. Each of Austin's brothers could've died at different points in the past nine months. As a result, Austin found he had a new appreciation for life and family. It was most likely the baby boom at the ranch that had him feeling soft, or the fact that he couldn't put to rest his feelings for Maria O'Brien, soon to be Belasco again, that made him resolve to talk to her and see if they could give their marriage another chance. He missed her and he was still scratching his head over what had happened to make her walk out.

Sure, they'd been through a rough patch, but wasn't that true of every relationship? He and Maria had never really had a big fight, a final blow to know they were both throwing in the towel. And then, divorce papers had arrived a couple of weeks ago. With everything going on at the ranch, he'd been too busy to look them over.

"How are you really feeling?" Austin asked Tommy.

"About as good as you look, so like a cow that just spent twenty hours in labor," Tommy teased.

"That good, huh? Well, some people just take a vacation when they want to lay in bed and watch TV for a few days instead of taking a bullet and rolling in via ambulance here at the Bluff Resort and Spa." Austin waved his arm in the air. "What time does the massage therapist come?"

"She'll be here any minute, so don't get too comfortable. And, by the way, she has the hands of a goddess," Tommy fired back with a chuckle in between bites, keeping the joke alive.

It was good to see him awake and alert rather than overmedicated and with tubes sticking out of him. None of the brothers, Austin included, could shake a similar image of their parents from nine months ago in this very hospital where they'd died. A later autopsy revealed they'd been poisoned and Tommy didn't seem any closer to an arrest.

"Found this last night and thought of you." Austin fished in the pocket of his shirt for the plastic badge he'd worn when they were kids. He pulled it out and tossed it onto the tray table.

"Wow. How old is this?" Tommy picked up the child's toy and spun it through his fingers.

Austin shrugged. "What age were we when we decided to become sheriffs?"

"Couldn't have been more than nine years old, right?"

"It was long before either one of us had hair on our chest, that's for sure," Austin said with a laugh. He couldn't imagine being anything other than a cattle rancher, although his childhood had been filled with the usual cop, fireman and Batman fantasies.

"Where on earth did you find this?" Tommy held the badge flat on his palm.

"Been in the top drawer of my desk," Austin said with a shrug.

"You never could throw anything away." Tommy examined the toy. "Good thing you went up north to that fancy school instead of law enforcement. I'm pretty sure your accounting skills are needed at the ranch more than your rifle acumen."

Going to a school in the Northeast had netted Austin the nickname Ivy League.

"Between you and Joshua, I figured the family was well represented in the badge-toting department," Austin said, referring to his brother who had left the ranch and moved to Denver to pursue a career in law enforcement. He returned over Christmas to take his rightful place alongside his brothers and had the toughest time adjusting.

Austin's cell buzzed. He fished it out of his jeans pocket and checked the screen. The text from his oldest brother, Dallas, read, Another calf is sick. Putting her in the pen.

"Everything okay?" Tommy asked, his gaze fixed on Austin's phone cover.

"Fine. Got some kind of sickness moving through the new stock. Half a dozen calves are isolated and under quarantine. Vet can't figure out what's going on and we're taking a wait-and-see approach for now. Hoping it doesn't get any worse," Austin stated.

Tommy didn't look away from the honeymoon picture of Austin and his wife that she'd had made into a phone cover. *Soon to be ex-wife*, an annoying little voice in the back of his mind corrected.

The look on Tommy's face sent a thousand fire ants crawling up Austin's spine.

"What is it?" he asked.

Tommy took a minute to speak and when he did, he fixed his gaze on a spot on the wall behind Austin. More reasons to be worried.

"Hey, Ivy League, do you remember Deputy Garretson?" Tommy finally asked.

"Yeah, sure. Why?" Garretson was a year ahead of Austin in school, so Dallas knew him better. Austin was the second-oldest O'Brien. The former deputy had moved to the capital a couple years back craving more day-to-day excitement than Bluff,

Texas, had to offer. He should've stuck around, Austin thought, because there'd been more than enough activity in the past year to keep him busy.

"He stopped by to see me yesterday," Tommy said and then paused.

"Everything okay with him?" Austin asked.

"He's fine," Tommy said quickly. "He's a detective now at Austin PD. Hangs out with his FBI liaison after work sometimes. Both are big Cowboys fans so they catch games together, grab a few beers."

Tommy was normally a straight-to-the-point guy. That he felt the need to dance around a topic didn't sit well with Austin. There was also a reference to the FBI, which was Maria's employer.

"What does this have to do with me?" Austin asked outright. Also a straight shooter.

"This guy, Special Agent DeCarlo, who Garretson buddies around with, is planning his wedding." Tommy's gaze bounced from the phone to Austin. He hesitated again before he spoke but he didn't need to say the words. Austin already knew what Tommy was about to say.

"He's planning to marry Maria."

DENALI, THE FAMILY'S Chocolate Lab, had been working alongside Austin for the better part of the night. Now, the hundred pound dog lay next to Austin's boots, panting and whimpering in his sleep. Austin would give a nickel to find out what went on in that dog's brain. *Never mind*, he thought wryly. Denali probably thought about food, treats and getting his ears scratched.

Austin pushed back from his desk and rubbed blurry eyes, thinking a few hours of shut-eye was a good idea considering how punchy he was getting. Between a record number of calves being born this winter and a bout of some kind of sickness causing him to quarantine half a dozen of them now, Austin had been working overtime for months. After learning his parents' deaths were being investigated as murders, he wasn't sleeping, either.

The news about Maria he'd received from Tommy earlier had been as unexpected as a sucker punch in broad daylight. His brain refused to process it, like it somehow wouldn't exist if he kept it at arm's length. So far, the only emotion he could strongly identify when he allowed it to surface was anger.

Adding to his sour mood was the fact that there was constant wedding/baby/adoption planning going on at the ranch. All five of his brothers had newborns, newly adopted children and/or wedding plans in the works. He didn't begrudge his brothers their happiness. In fact, he was over the moon for them and each was the happiest he'd ever seen. They'd found true love, fought for it, and had earned the reward of real partners in life and that was great. Personally, he was on the opposite end of the spectrum as divorce papers stared at him from the corner pile of paperwork on his desk and his wife made wedding plans with another man.

The papers had been sitting there for a while now. Austin had lost track of how many days. A dozen? More? The thought of signing them had proved harder than he'd expected, so he kept putting off the task. He should probably be glad to end that chapter of his life and move on, good riddance and all. Maria had made her decision clear and he wasn't one to stand in her way.

That familiar mix of anger and heartache cut through his chest as he made a move to pick up the legal document. He stopped midreach. He'd been staring at the laptop so long that his eyes were practically crossed and every letter on the screen was a haze. Numbers ran together like highway signs at a hundred miles an hour, a blurry streak. His brain was toast. He wanted to be in the right mind-set before looking over those papers and make sure he had time to read the fine print.

On second thought, a signature could wait. A few more days wouldn't make a difference in either of their lives. The annoying voice in the back of his mind said that wasn't exactly true for Maria. Austin shoved the thought aside. The clock read half past eleven. He'd be up again at four thirty sharp, an unholy hour for a natural night owl like him. He needed a hot shower and a firm mattress. The news from Tommy about Maria had knocked Austin off balance and all he needed was a little rest to get his emotions in check. That little piece of him that had said it wasn't over between them yet—that they still had a chance as long as they were still married—had been shattered all to hell. It wasn't Tommy's fault. He was trying to protect Austin from finding out through a different source. O'Briens were news. The story would be out soon enough. Anything to do with his family made headlines.

Austin picked up his cell that had been sitting on top of his desk and looked at the picture on his phone cover. He and Maria had been so happy, or so he'd believed. How could any of it have been real if she was willing to throw it away so easily? And for what? Because the pregnancy didn't work out? Yes, it had been a difficult time for both of them. He'd retreated into himself and had shut down. He could be honest and admit that now. Maria had started spending longer hours on her caseload at the FBI. Then, a few weeks later when the doctor had cleared them to try again, she'd said that she reconsidered the timing of having children. The timing was right for her to go for the promotion into the Crimes Against Children program, saying it had been a job she'd always wanted. News to him, he'd thought. She'd pointed out that they were still young and had plenty of time to start their family. In hindsight, he should've picked up on the oversell.

Austin had figured that she was saying she needed a little more time to get over what had happened. So he gave her what she'd asked for, what he'd believed she needed: time and space.

Neither had worked out so well.

It had become easier to stay apart than to face each other and try to build a bridge to cover the space between them. He'd started spending more time in the barn and on the range. The divide between them became a cavern until she'd rented a loft apartment in the capital to be closer to work and then stopped coming home altogether.

A dull ache pounded Austin's temples as if a dozen hammers were a marching band in his ears. Sleep. He needed a few hours of shut-eye before the day started over again. He'd been working so much lately that days and nights ran together and he lost track of the calendar. He'd rest come July when he got the healthy calves sold at auction. Right now, the sick calves deserved his attention.

"Let's go, boy," he said to Denali, who'd stopped whining and was settled into a pattern of steady breathing.

The Lab didn't so much as hike an ear at the sound of Austin's voice. A good cattle dog was worth three men. Denali did his own thing, which generally meant sleeping a lot. But he was good company and he'd been in the family fourteen years.

"Okay, old man," Austin said, figuring he could keep the door to his office open so Denali could come and go as he pleased when he woke, like usual. The dog liked to roam around, stopping in to visit who he wanted each day.

Austin maintained his workplace in the horse barn to be closer to the men. His father had occupied the big office next door. Austin stopped in front of Dad's office. The room was dark and empty now.

Since the murders, no one had claimed the big office as theirs, as though everyone realized there'd be no filling the boots of their father.

Austin took in a sharp breath.

"You stay here and rest," Austin said to the snoring Lab, thinking that he sorely needed to get out and socialize again in the summer since he'd taken to talking to the family dog more than people. Of course, most sane people didn't wake up before the sun.

Austin hopped onto the bench seat of the golf cart and headed east toward his home. The place had been constructed almost a decade ago. His had been the first built on the ranch because he'd always known he'd come back to work the land he loved after college. Yeah, Tommy was right, Austin had gone to a fancy school. And he needed every bit of his Ivy League education to carry the ranch into the next generation and beyond.

Winding down the path beside the flowing water of Bull Creek, Austin noticed how the water flowed through the land, always moving. He stopped the cart next to the creek, stepped out and listened to the rush of water.

His thoughts drifted back to Maria. Smart, beautiful, focused. She'd been everything he'd ever wanted in a relationship and so much more. That first year they'd stayed up long past a reasonable time every night talking. His mornings might've dragged the next day but he'd do it all over again the next because he wanted to be with her that much. Her good looks had attracted him. She was a classic brown-haired, brown-eyed beauty. But it was her intelligence that rocketed his attraction to a whole new dimension. And the sex…he didn't even want to go there about how mind-blowing that had been. No doubt a product of the intensity of the emotions they felt for each other.

Austin stood over the water, watching it flow. He shook his head, wondering how he could've let their relationship slip through his fingers.

Back inside the cart, he let the word he'd been avoiding circulate through his thoughts…*divorce*.

It sat heavy on his chest as he stood in front of the locked door of his traditional ranch-style home, remembering that he'd left the key back at his office on top of the divorce papers.

Chapter Two

Still half-asleep, Austin groaned at the noise waking him. The music needed to stop. Instead, Johnny Cash's song "Ring of Fire" belted out louder. Austin was pretty sure his eyelids had been glued shut at some point in the night as he moved in slow motion. He forcibly blinked his eyes open, searching for the culprit. The clock on his nightstand said two forty in the morning. And he realized the annoying sound was his ringtone.

He shot straight up. His first thought was that something had happened to Tommy, so he scrambled to answer before the call rolled into the black abyss of voice mail where he couldn't ask important questions.

"Is this Austin O'Brien?" an unfamiliar female voice said.

"Yes, ma'am."

She identified herself as Maureen Velasquez from University Medical Center. "We got your number from Maria O'Brien's emergency contact in her phone and we need your consent to treat her."

"What happened? Hold on. Can I give it to you over the phone?" A next-of-kin call from University Medical Center's trauma unit asking for his permission to treat his wife was the last discussion Austin thought he'd have after being served divorce papers. Technically, she was still Maria O'Brien but that would change to Belasco as soon as he signed the documents on his desk. Apparently, another change was on the horizon for her soon after. That thought sat bitterly in Austin's gut. It was a lot like rusted metal lodged in there, metallic taste and all.

"I'm afraid it has to be in writing," Maureen said sympathetically.

"Is she okay?" he asked, trying to process being up after three hours of sleep, and then said, "Never mind. You have my verbal consent and I'll be right there to sign whatever document you need. My lawyer will call in the meantime."

"Thank you, sir," Maureen said. "I'll meet you at the ER entrance with the paperwork."

Austin ended the call and tore off the covers. He hopped into his jeans and threw on a shirt. He slipped into his boots and was out the door within minutes.

The drive to the hospital was the longest of his life. He probably should've expected this call to come at some point given the nature of her job. Except that Maria was probably the most competent person he'd ever known and he'd never given much thought to the danger in her line of work. Not until right then. And now every possible worst-case scenario was running through his mind. He should've asked Maureen more questions when he had her on the line but he didn't want to take a chance of delaying treatment.

Other thoughts churned in his mind—thoughts that he couldn't afford now that Maria was divorcing him. Austin needed a strong black cup of coffee to clear his mind and reset those thoughts.

He left his truck next to the ER ambulance bay, having parked on the side so emergency vehicles had plenty of room. A woman in slacks and a button-down shirt stood at the entrance with a clipboard tucked under her arm.

"Ms. Velasquez?" he asked and she nodded as she held out the clipboard.

"Sign here, Mr. O'Brien," she said, indicating a spot at the bottom of the page.

He scribbled his name as quickly as he could.

"And here," she flipped up the document to reveal a page underneath as she nodded to a nurse who was standing at the intake desk on the phone. Austin assumed the nurse was relaying the fact that they had consent. The speed at which they handled everything sent a chill down his back. This couldn't be good.

"Your wife is being taken into surgery to stitch up the back of her head," Maureen stated, and her voice was calm, even.

"She's going to be all right, though, isn't she?"

Austin asked, not wanting to let his fears get the best of him.

"We have the best trauma doctors in the country, Mr. O'Brien. Your wife is in good hands," Maureen said, indicating a third place for his signature.

When he'd signed, he searched her face for any indication that she was placating him. She seemed sincere.

"I'll take you to a waiting area where you can find a decent cup of coffee," she said. "Someone will be out to talk to you the minute your wife is out of surgery."

"What happened?"

"She was alone, believed to be walking to her car when she took a blow to the head from behind," she supplied.

"How bad is it?" he asked.

"The doctor is with her now and he'll be able to give you a full report." She shot him an apologetic look.

"Where was she when this happened?"

"Outside of a place called Midnight Cowboy, on Sixth Street," she supplied. "An employee came out the back door and the guy supposedly took off before she could get a good look at him."

Austin thanked her and followed her down the long white hallway.

She opened a door to a lounge, closed the door behind him, and it didn't take but another minute for him to get started on that first cup.

There were a few people in the waiting area, scattered around, some in pairs. The thought that he might be in the same room with the man who planned to marry his wife was a bitter pill to swallow. Austin scanned each male face to see if he recognized any of the men or if any one of them seemed like someone Maria would date.

There was one contender, a man in his midthirties, fairly stocky for what had to be about a five-foot-ten-inch frame. The guy was sitting off to the side by himself. He wore camo pants and a dark green T-shirt, fairly typical FBI field clothing. His elbows rested on his knees, and his right foot hadn't stopped fidgeting since Austin had stepped into the room. The man could be worried about Maria or tense about meeting her husband, Austin thought wryly. He leaned against the wall, needing to stand for a few minutes while he sipped his coffee. Besides, the dark blue chairs lining the walls looked about as hard and itchy as sitting on a bale of hay.

The haze in his brain started lifting and he convinced himself that he'd stick around long enough to make sure Maria was in the clear and out of surgery. She may not even want him there. Camo Pants might be the one getting the nod to see her when she woke.

Anger filled his chest as he thought about how easy it seemed for her to be able to replace their relationship. For him, what they'd had was special. Apparently, not so much for her.

News that she was in recovery came two cups

of coffee and little more than one hour later. Austin took it as a good sign. Camo Pants didn't make a move when the doctor stepped into the doorway and asked to speak to Austin O'Brien. Austin double-checked Camo Pants for a reaction when the doctor said Maria's name, too. He didn't get one. Good. Austin wasn't sure how he'd react if his replacement was sitting in the same room.

It struck him as odd that her fiancé wouldn't be notified. But then, that was just paperwork.

Austin followed the doctor into the hall so they could speak one-on-one. After hearing medical-lingo for Maria was doing better than expected due to her strong physical condition, Austin asked how long she could expect to be in the hospital.

"Not long. Cognitively, she's doing far better than expected," the middle-aged doctor, who looked committed to a workout routine himself, said. He'd introduced himself as Dr. Burt and had a tired but competent look to his graying features. "A blow to the head like the one she took can scramble things up. Her mind seems clear. She knew her name and the day of the week. She also knew the current president and vice president."

Austin didn't know how to put this delicately, so he came straight out with it. "We're going through a divorce, so I'm not sure if it's appropriate for me to stick around much longer. I'd like to know that she'll recover fully before I leave, though."

"Leave?" The doctor's brow shot up. "You were

the first person she asked to see when she woke. She asked for her husband."

Again, the delicate way to approach this seemed to take leave so Austin asked point-blank, "Are you sure she's talking about me?"

"You're Austin O'Brien, correct?" Dr. Burt asked.

"I am."

"Then I'm absolutely talking about you," he said.

"And she didn't mention anything about sending me divorce papers or planning to marry someone else?"

"No." A concerned crease dented the doctor's forehead. "In fact, she seemed excited about heading back to the ranch with you."

"The ranch?" Austin's reaction seemed to catch the doctor off guard.

"She doesn't live with you on your family ranch?" he asked.

Austin shook his head and worry lines bracketed Dr. Burt's mouth.

"You said she took a blow to the head," Austin said, fearing that she might've taken a bigger hit than they realized.

Dr. Burt nodded. "Short-term memory loss can be an issue with a head injury. I'll set up a meeting with you and the nurse to check the accuracy of the information she provided. If she doesn't live with you, where does she live?"

"She moved to an apartment in Austin more than a year ago," Austin said honestly. He didn't really want to get into the shortcomings of his relationship with his wife but it sounded like information they needed to treat her properly. He could get through a few uncomfortable minutes if it would help.

The doctor's frown deepened. "Interesting. She didn't mention anything about it." He paused. "I'll contact our trauma specialist for a consult and, if you don't mind, I'd like for you to be available for an interview, as well."

"I'll do what I can to help," he said, unsure if he was the right person for the task.

Dr. Burt deposited Austin in a small office and then left, saying he'd return soon. The doctor's words sent all of Austin's warning flags flying at high altitude.

A few minutes passed before the door opened again and a white-haired doctor stepped inside.

"I'm Dr. Wade." This doctor was a little shorter than Dr. Burt with a few more wrinkles.

The interview didn't last as long as Austin's cup of coffee.

"I'd like to confer with my colleague before making a recommendation," he said, pausing at the door.

Austin thanked him and waited.

Three hours later, Dr. Burt stepped inside the room. "My shift is almost over but I wanted to speak to you personally before I left."

"I appreciate it," Austin said.

"Your wife is in recovery and doing well. After speaking to her, it's safe to say that she's suffering memory loss from the trauma her head received," the doctor began, taking a seat across from Austin. "The blow was severe enough to cause some swelling to the brain."

"Sounds serious," Austin said, tamping down his fear that the doctor was about to deliver life-changing news.

"We'll have to monitor her for the next twenty-four to forty-eight hours but I'm hopeful for a positive outcome given her otherwise strong physical condition," Dr. Burt said.

"And what about her memory?" Austin asked.

"That's where it gets complicated. There are two basic types of amnesia, retrograde and anterograde," Dr. Burt started. He leaned forward and touched the tips of his fingers together. "Amnesia is simple. We all know what that means. We had a memory once and now it's gone." He snapped his fingers for emphasis. "The memory is lost."

Straightforward enough. Austin nodded his understanding.

"Anterograde amnesia erases short-term memories following an accident or trauma and a good part of that is due to injury to the brain itself. Chemicals shift and the balance is disturbed. Once that brain chemistry normalizes, systems work again." He folded his fingers together. "Had a guy released last week who'd spent four months here but can't recall anything before the last week of his stay."

"Will those memories come back for him?" Austin asked after taking a sip of coffee that he'd refilled prior to the doctor entering the room.

"Maybe. Maybe not." Dr. Burt made a seesaw effect with outstretched arms. "I've seen it go both ways.

"With retrograde amnesia, like in your wife's case—" he paused "—a patient loses memories of events before the injury. For some, the loss will cover a few minutes. Others can lose weeks, months or even years of their lives. I've personally witnessed both ends of the spectrum."

"What about Maria?" Austin asked, absorbing the news. His first thought was that the only reason she'd asked for him was because she didn't remember that she'd been the one to walk away in the first place. And what did any of that mean for their relationship? Was he supposed to forget the fact that she'd served him with divorce papers and pretend like nothing was wrong?

"It's difficult to say at this point. Memories have a tendency to return like pieces in a jigsaw puzzle. They'll get bits here and there with no rhyme or reason," Dr. Burt said.

"Is it a permanent condition? Can it come and go?" Austin asked. What he knew about amnesia could fill his coffee cup and nothing more. And most of that knowledge came from him or one of his brothers suffering from a concussion in childhood.

"Many people regain much of what they've lost, if not all. For some, they never retrieve that information. The brain is complicated and there's not a one-size-fits-all approach." Dr. Burt's shoulders relaxed. He maintained soft eye contact, blinking and looking away as he recalled information. Everything about the man's posture communicated compassion. "If it's any consolation, we've observed a direct correlation between recovery of the head injury and return of memories. The better the healing, the more long-term memories tend to come back."

"I'm guessing you can't tell me when that will happen," Austin said.

"Not with any degree of confidence," the doctor admitted. "Generally speaking, the less severe the head injury, the smaller the degree of associated retrograde amnesia. From evaluating her memory versus the trauma to her head, I'd guess that her memories could return fairly soon. She's in excellent physical condition and that always aids recovery. Her head sustained a fair amount of trauma both from the blunt force instrument and then when she fell after the initial blow. Indications are that she collided hard with the concrete. That being said, she's young and strong. Both of those factors weigh in. The better she takes care of herself in recovery, the more hopeful I am."

"Will this affect her ability to do her job?" Austin asked.

"She won't be able to go back to work without medical clearance," Dr. Burt said. "We'll recommend follow-up treatment as part of her rehabilitation plan."

"What about forcing reality? Can I tell her the truth about our life?" he asked.

"That's up to you." He clasped his hands.

"She might not want to see me when she remembers the past," Austin admitted.

"This has to be a difficult situation for you. If you care about her, my advice is to take it easy. Making memories flood back before the brain can handle them can cause even more distress and delay her progress," Dr. Burt stated. "I'm sorry. I'm sure that's not news you wanted to hear."

Austin needed to ask another question. He wasn't sure he wanted to know the answer except that experience had taught him that dodging a problem usually made it worse. That was especially true with his marriage. He would have to face the music that she was involved with another man at some point. "She didn't mention wanting to see anyone else, did she?"

"No." Dr. Burt looked Austin square in the eye. "It seems like your situation is—" the doctor searched the white floor tile like the answer might be found there "—complicated. No one would blame you for walking away. You signed the paperwork consenting treatment, so you've done your part. She'll likely recover her memory in a few days, possibly weeks, and if there's someone else in her life, then you might not want to be around for the moment she remembers him and wants him to be the one to help her."

The man had a point.

"Thanks for the honesty and for everything you've done for her," Austin said, knowing full well that he couldn't walk away until he knew that Maria would be okay. He hadn't expected the call to come in the first place. He hadn't expected to spend the next two nights at a bedside vigil, pretending to be something they were not, a happy couple. And least of all, he hadn't expected to be the one taking her to her apartment to settle in, a place he'd never set foot in—the place where she'd moved to get away from him.

But there he was, doing it all the same.

Maria was smart, athletic and strong. Seeing her in a hospital bed, helpless, with tubes sticking out of her had been a blow that had knocked Austin back a few steps. Divorce or not, he needed to see her get back on her feet.

There was another kink. Even though she'd been cleared of her head injury, she made no progress on regaining her memories. She didn't remember the fact that they were separated let alone on the verge of divorce. Austin had expected her fiancé to drop by at some point during the hospital stay. He'd been told on the second day that Dr. Burt had convinced him, whoever *he* was, to stay away for now.

Maria was quiet on the ride to her loft.

Stepping inside, she seemed as lost as he felt.

"Funny, I don't remember this place as much as I do our house on the ranch," Maria said, those big brown eyes of hers staring up at him as he stood in the unfamiliar surroundings of the open-concept loft. "And why do I have an apartment here in Austin away from you anyway?"

The doctor had said that her memories could come back one at a time or as an avalanche. One at a time was the best scenario, he'd said.

"To be closer to work," Austin said, not feeling a connection to the city where she lived even though he shared its name. Lies were racking up. The doctor had said that Maria was most likely suppressing negative memories and that it was best to let her mind work everything out.

Give her time, he'd said. *She'll come around.*

"Why don't I see any of your things? Don't you live here, too?" she asked, glancing around as she took a step toward the kitchen island.

"I'm needed on the ranch," he said, shaking his head.

Talking to Maria like nothing was wrong, like those damn papers weren't sitting on his desk waiting to be signed, seemed like an even worse betrayal than the day she'd walked out.

Chapter Three

"Can I sit here? I'm not really tired enough to go to bed." Maria motioned toward the couch. "Besides, I've already been lying down for what feels like an eternity."

Austin put his arm around her waist, ignoring the electricity pinging between them as he helped her to the sofa. She leaned into him and, for a second, he remembered how good her body was at molding to his. How soft her skin was…

Those thoughts were as productive as shoveling mulch with a pitchfork.

She eased down with a groan. Austin didn't need to think it was sexy. But her voice had always had that effect on him.

Her long brown hair parted on the side now and fell way past her shoulders. She'd grown it out since he'd last seen her. And he was certain a lot of other things had changed about her since then, too.

"I never knew this many places in my body could hurt at the same time," she said with a quick smile.

Austin forced his gaze away from her rosy lips.

"If you'd take stronger pain medicine like the doctor prescribed, you wouldn't have to suffer." Austin didn't want to notice how toned that body of hers was. Her work as a special agent would ensure she stayed in tip-top physical condition. And the truth was that she loved to exercise.

"Then how will I know when I'm doing damage to something?" she asked with those big brown eyes staring at him. After she made herself comfortable, she beamed up at him and then grabbed his hand and tugged him toward her. "Besides, all those pills do is make me nauseous anyway."

Austin straightened his back and pulled out of her grip, stuffing his hand inside his jeans pocket instead. His muscles corded with tension. He didn't need to go there with the being-her-comfort thing. "You want anything to drink? Water?"

"Coffee sounds good." She looked at him blankly and a little hurt. He'd spent the past two days at her side in the hospital, pretending that everything was fine. No doubt she had questions as he started to pull back. There was a mix of confusion and hurt in her eyes that he wished wasn't his fault. Austin didn't like putting it there but he couldn't risk getting too close this time. He had to protect himself, too. Soon enough she'd remember that she'd gotten tired of their marriage, had classified it as a youthful mistake, and then had walked out.

Were it not for being Texan and a gentleman, he

wouldn't be here in the first place. Call it Cowboy Code or whatever but Austin couldn't refuse someone who truly needed his help, especially not someone he'd cared about. And that's as far as he could allow feelings for Maria Belasco to go.

His ringtone sounded, belting Johnny Cash's "Ring of Fire" and her face lit up. She no doubt remembered it was the song that had been playing the first time they'd met at the Cash Fest, one of the many charity events his mother had organized that had been centered around the man's music and benefited rising talent.

Austin fished out his cell, grunted, and then turned to walk away. It was his brother Dallas on the line. Austin would call him back.

"Want to put on some music?" Maria asked, and her voice was loaded with unasked questions.

The two of them had connected on a lot of levels but the first thing that really got him was her love of the blues, rockabilly and country music. He'd play some obscure bluegrass song, and she'd know what it was. And then there was their shared love of the same books. In the back of Austin's pickup was a dog-eared copy of *The Old Man and the Sea*, his all-time favorite story. Turns out that it was Maria's, too. On top of having music and literature in common, she was determined, brilliant…and beautiful.

"I finished reading that book you gave me. *Happens to Be Real.*" She motioned toward the rectangular coffee table in front of her.

Austin tensed. He didn't know what to make of the fact that she kept the last book he'd lent her on the coffee table of the apartment she shared with another man. Although, a cursory glance didn't reveal any men's items at the loft. He shouldn't feel relieved but no man wanted his nose rubbed in the fact that his ex was involved in a new relationship.

"Are we not on good terms?" she asked, and there was an innocent quality to her voice that threatened to put a chink in his armor.

Not so fast. She'd always been perceptive and he'd have to be less transparent if this was going to work.

"We're okay," he said with a shrug, wondering how much he should tell her. For a second, he thought about throwing out the adage that all married couples go through ups and downs and the two of them had been on a downswing. He reconsidered, not wanting to jar her memory too fast. "Nothing major."

"Good. I was beginning to worry there for a second," she said, and he could tell that she was going along with him while she studied the situation. Being astute had helped her rise up the ranks quickly at the Bureau.

Austin needed that coffee. *Now.*

"Sorry if I'm sending mixed signals. We have sick calves at the ranch and we're trying to figure out what's going on and just how many are affected. I haven't been sleeping much in the last few weeks, longer than that if I'm honest." It seemed enough information to satisfy her arched brow without causing an avalanche of questions he wasn't supposed to answer.

Austin moved into the adjacent kitchen. The space was small but had all the essentials, including a microwave and coffee machine. Other than that, the loft was fairly bare.

There was a couch and matching chair in the living area nestled around a wooden coffee table that looked handmade. Barstools pushed up to the island in the kitchen must be where she ate all her meals since there wasn't a dining table and chairs. A long, narrow table was pushed against the wall near the door with a bowl on it for miscellaneous items like car keys. There was a pair of running shoes at the door, so she still must wake before the cows to get in her morning run before work. Relief he had no right to own washed over Austin that there weren't a pair of men's shoes tucked next to hers. For a second, he wondered if Dr. Burt had instructed the new guy to erase his presence from her loft so as not to confuse her.

Adding to his theory was the fact that there were no other signs of a male presence in the place so far. No picture frames. No visible clothing, although he hadn't been in the bathroom yet because they'd just left the hospital. Other than a lamp and a bowl, there was nothing on the table by the door to indicate she'd settled into the place. A few unpacked boxes had been pushed against one corner. The place was open concept so he could see the bed positioned in the middle of the bedroom space. Thankfully, the only clothes he could see so far were Maria's.

"Did we move in here recently?" she asked, and she must've been watching him take in the space.

"This is your place in the city for those long nights at work," he said without making eye contact.

She seemed satisfied with the answer or at least she didn't press for more information.

"Did the doctor say when I can get back to work?" she asked as he made coffee.

Figures her first real worry would be about the job. He'd blame all their problems on her dedication to the FBI if he thought that would make him feel better. It wouldn't. What rubbed him was the fact that she'd allowed the miscarriage to break up their marriage. No trying again. No talking about it. She'd grown distant, said it would never work between them, and then stopped coming home.

Austin stared at the bottom of an empty coffee cup. He filled it and then a second one with the warm brown liquid.

"You still take two sugars?" he asked, instantly realizing his mistake. He muttered a curse. He was no good at deception. Ranchers had the benefit of living an honest life. Not really a skill that would benefit him in this situation, he thought wryly.

Her brow arched as she nodded.

Austin could've kicked himself. This was going to be more difficult than he originally suspected. If playing house could help her avoid serious trauma, he'd do his level best no matter how dishonest he felt. He reminded himself of the tough childhood she'd had. Losing her mother in the way that she had, blaming herself in the way that she did. She carried a tough burden on her shoulders and he could do this if he really put his mind to it.

"Yeah," she said with a concerned look on her face as she took the mug being offered.

He needed to give her a better explanation about their circumstances or risk stressing her out further.

"You've been working a lot," he said, and that was partially true. "We haven't spent much time together in the past year."

"Oh. Okay. I sensed that something was going on," she said, taking a sip of fresh brew and making a mewling noise. "This is amazing."

Austin tried not to think about a similar sound that drew from her throat in the moments before she exploded around him when they made love.

"Yeah, it's good," was all he managed to say.

"It's strange that I live here and yet I don't re-member this place," she said. "I wish we could go home to the ranch."

"It's too far from the hospital and your doctors, remember?" he said, not wanting to read too much into the fact that the only place she remembered as home was his ranch. The doctor had said that head trauma could do strange things to a person.

One thing was certain, with the baby boom going on at the ranch, he couldn't take her there. He wouldn't risk all her memories crashing down around her triggered by the reason for the distance between them in the first place. The doctor had said that her brain would unlock pieces of reality as she renewed her daily routine. Anything else could be too fast, too traumatic. And Austin was certain that seeing their daughter's nursery would release a flood.

As much as Austin didn't like the idea of playing house at her loft, he could hang in there for a few more days. The place wasn't exactly homey but there were enough essentials here to survive. All he really needed was a coffee maker and microwave, and she had both. Maria had never been much of a cook, which had never bothered Austin. They both knew enough to get by and had had more kitchen sex than probably any other room because of it. But great sex wasn't the only thing he missed about her. He missed her quick wit, her sharp sense of humor, the way she'd seemed to understand him without even needing to talk. How did everything get so messed up between them? How had it come to this?

"I'm still a little unclear as to how I ended up in the hospital," she said.

"You were jumped from behind," he said. "And the guy caught you off guard."

"Was I working?" she asked.

"No. You were off the clock and had stopped off to meet with friends." Austin didn't say that she was having a draft beer at the Midnight Cowboy on Sixth

Street after meeting up with a group of people, one of which was most likely the guy she planned to marry.

"Now that I think about it, I remember working a lot of late hours," she said, and then her gaze landed on him. He must've given a look without realizing it.

"What is it?" she asked.

"Nothing." He shrugged. When she wasn't in Austin she'd brought work home to the ranch with her. Her eyes had been glued to her laptop most of the time. He couldn't remember the last time he'd seen her relaxed, like now, and her dedication to her work had only escalated the tension between them. "What else do you remember?"

"Not much. But I have a question. I'm married to you and all I do is work?" She'd forgotten all the tension between them, all the times he'd busted out the back door after her at the ranch, not knowing what to say or do to make his wife happy again.

Austin took in a sharp breath. Lucky her.

"Things are a little more complicated than that but we don't have to talk about it right now," he said.

"Why not?" she asked. "I can't think of anything better to do."

"It's not important compared to what you're going through right now." It was the first honest thing he'd said since arriving at her place.

"Yeah, okay," she said, looking frustrated. Her hand came up to her forehead as if trying to recall was giving her a headache.

"You have to take it easy," he said, trying to soothe her without getting too close.

She looked up at him and half smiled. "You're right. I'm sure it'll come back. It's just hard when it feels like everyone else knows things about my life that I don't."

The last doctor he'd spoken with at the university hospital had said that there was no physical reason for her memory loss. It was possible that her brain was suppressing anything it viewed as a difficult issue. If she saw being on the verge of finalizing their divorce as traumatic, her brain might just decide to push that into a shadow. Force it out and the ramifications could be overwhelming to her.

"Whatever's going on between us that's causing you stress, I want you to know that I'm sorry," she said with so much sincerity and sadness.

His hands fisted to stop from reaching out to her, to being her comfort. How many nights had he stayed awake, starting at the ceiling, wishing one of them could open up before she'd left? The memory burned a hole in Austin's chest. Remembering wasn't all it was cracked up to be.

"Don't worry about it." Focusing on the past wouldn't get them back on track with her healing. Once she got her memories back she wouldn't want to have anything to do with him again. "The most important thing for you to focus on is healing."

"Guess work can't come between us now," she

said, referring to the fact that she was being forced to take time off until she got medical clearance.

"True," Austin said. He meant to smile but couldn't seem to force it.

"What are you really worried about? The ranch? Is it really that bad there?" she asked. "And don't say it's me."

"We'll figure out what's going on with the calves. What makes you so sure I'm concerned about something other than your health?" He took a seat on the edge of the armchair and sipped his coffee.

"You always get this line across your forehead. It's deep because that's the way you care about things. Your eyes widen just a little and your irises get bigger, the opposite of what happens to most people," she said. "And you don't look me straight in the eye when you talk to me. All other times it's like you're seeing right through me and I can't stop wondering what happened to make it go away."

MARIA COULDN'T IMAGINE what had transpired between her and the handsome Austin O'Brien to make things seem so awkward at moments. But it had to be something serious. And he was covering up whatever it was. Maybe they were in the middle of a fight and he didn't want to bring it up or stir up negative memories? It would've had to be something bad for him to react to her so stiffly. She feared there was a whole lot more to the story of her moving into the loft. All of that was frustratingly patchy.

Even so, that's not what she remembered most about their relationship. There'd been a physical attraction, sure. His emerald green eyes, strong squared jaw and black-as-night tight-clipped hair were the first things she'd noticed about him. What had kept her coming back for more was his laid-back laugh, that infuriating sparkle to his eye that had melted her heart every time she looked at him and been so good at seducing her. And then there was the way it was so easy to be around him.

From the moment she'd met Austin, he just felt like home. And that was weird because she couldn't remember the last time she truly felt at home anywhere or with anyone before him.

And now it was just…off.

They'd shared so many similar interests in music and books. And then there was the way he made her laugh no matter how hard her day had been or how sour her mood when she walked through the door. Within minutes of being around him, her entire disposition changed. The stress of the day would disintegrate and a sense of calm, of being right where she was supposed to be, would settle over her.

Those were the things she remembered about being with him.

Another feeling was present now and it had nothing to do with the handsome, virile cowboy.

This was the sensation of someone or something lurking in the shadows, just out of sight, waiting…

She couldn't shake the hairs-standing-up-on-the-back-of-her-neck feeling no matter how hard she tried.

And she'd tried.

Chapter Four

Austin was hiding the truth from Maria. Her memories might be patchy but she knew him well enough to know that he'd been tap-dancing around something since the first day they'd come home from the hospital. He'd looked around the loft as though he'd never seen it before, which struck her as odd. Adding to her confusion, he'd insisted on checking out the bathroom before giving her access. He'd seemed so relieved when he turned from the doorjamb and told her it was clear. Clear from what?

Then, there were the sleeping arrangements. He'd said that he slept like a tornado and didn't want to risk rolling over onto her in the night. So, he'd taken the couch since they'd arrived, which was three nights ago.

Fast-forward to today. Austin was out picking up dinner and Maria was grateful that he'd left. He was probably just worried about her but he kept watch over her like she was a China doll about to tip off the top shelf and shatter. He was just worried about her, she reasoned. That had to be the reason that he hadn't made an attempt to touch her...*right*?

Because she remembered that the heat between the two of them could've melted a glacier and now all she got was a cold shoulder.

Maria leaned her head against the rolled-up hand towel as she stretched out her sore legs. The bathwater was the perfect temperature and the jets pulsed at just the right speed to untangle her tense muscles. Another twenty minutes of this and she'd be good to go.

Maria glanced at the clock. Austin should be back soon. She'd spent an extra ten minutes soaking and was starting to feel human again thanks to the pair of ibuprofen she'd swallowed before getting in the water. She turned off the jets and then opened the drain.

The tile floor was cold on her bare feet and a chill raced through her. Her clothes were in a pile on the floor in front of the sink. She had to step over them to reach her towel. As she lifted her right foot, she heard a sizzling sound. It was like droplets of water on a hot griddle.

Her gaze flew to the spot where an accompanying hissing sound vibrated. Her T-shirt moved and that couldn't be a good sign. Something was underneath there. The bathroom walls seemed to shrink as the sizzling sound grew louder. She withdrew her foot and hopped back into the tub immediately. She slipped, almost bit it, and had to regain her balance by grabbing hold of the sides of the tub.

She froze as a diamond-shaped head with a pair of beady eyes and a forked tongue peeked out from underneath her T-shirt. The second it made eye contact her pulse raced and the sizzling noise vibrated. One strike could cover the distance between them, and she'd be dead before Austin could bring her fish tacos back from her favorite restaurant, Pescado.

Maria had never been terrified of anyone, not even the boogeyman when she was a little girl. But she was deathly afraid of snakes.

Her body ached from crouching low. It was the same defensive maneuver she would use in any threatening scenario, put as much mass between her and the enemy as possible. If that double-eyed monster made a move, at least the bathtub was between them save for half of her head.

Her tired legs might give out and she didn't dare move an inch or risk agitating the creature. This was the perfect time to remember that her gun was in the other room, she thought as she rolled her eyes. Even if she had her weapon she couldn't just randomly shoot in the middle of her building. A stray bullet could kill an innocent person and she wouldn't want to risk it.

Unfortunately, her cell was in the other room, too. She hadn't thought to bring it with her into the bathroom. Then again, she hadn't expected to need it.

Maria cursed under her breath, praying that Austin would make it home before the deadly snake launched toward her. As it was she could hear her own heartbeat pounding inside her ears.

At least for now the sizzling noises had quieted. No way did she plan to take her eyes off that thing or relax. She remembered reading somewhere that most snakes could strike at least two-thirds of their body length, depending on the type and size. Most of this one's body was hidden, so she had no idea how long it was. She had no plans to find out or test the theory, either.

Noise came from the other room…and the T-shirt moved.

AUSTIN SET THE BAG of take-out fish tacos on the kitchen island when he heard a noise, a strangled cry, from the bathroom.

His pulse kicked up and he ate up the real estate between him and the sound in a couple of strides. As he placed his hand on the knob, Maria said, "Don't come in."

He started to tap on the door with a knuckled fist instead.

"Don't make a sound, Austin," Maria pleaded.

Didn't that get all his warning bells flaring. He pressed an ear to the door to see if he could figure out what the hell was going on. At first, he didn't pick up anything.

And then he heard something…a sizzling noise.

Austin dropped to the floor effortlessly, without

making a sound. His white Stetson landed with a soft thud on the floor next to him and he bit back a curse. All he could see clearly was a pile of clothes in front of the sink. The tub was to the left and out of range at this vantage point.

And then he saw something—a snake. From the back, he could see that the head was small but marked with a prominent dark brown arrow-shape. Austin knew exactly what kind of snake he was dealing with, a saw-scaled viper. Dangerous. Aggressive. Deadly. Known for its lightning-fast strike and powerful venom. The viper was moving backward, away from the threat, and his brown body was partially covered underneath Maria's T-shirt.

The sizzling noise made sense. This kind of viper rubbed its scales together to create a warning sound. Austin needed to distract attention away from Maria without getting himself bit. Thinking about how snakes had been her only hesitation at moving to the ranch when they'd first married, he didn't need her panicking. Not much could rattle Maria. Snakes were her wake-up-in-the-middle-of-the-night-in-a-cold-sweat fear.

If he spoke, the snake would immediately redirect toward him, but aggravating it could prove deadly for Maria since she was trapped in the bathroom with it. He pushed up, moved away from the door and sat. What could he use to trap it?

Austin moved around the loft, searching for something—*anything*, making as little noise as humanly possible. He muttered a curse under his breath when he didn't see a thing he could use. He was losing precious time. One wrong move and Maria could end up fighting for her life. Anger roared through him.

In the corner of the bedroom area, he spotted something that might work. He picked up the wicker weave laundry basket with burlap lining and then tested its strength. This should hold.

Heart in this throat, he moved to the bathroom door. Dropping onto all fours, he pressed his head to the floor. The snake was almost up against the adjacent wall. He gripped the rim of the basket tighter, turning it upside down.

Here went nothing...

In one motion, he opened the door as the snake launched. It struck the door and recoiled. Austin held steady for a three-count, stepped inside, and then closed the door.

The viper struck again and hit the inside rim of the basket.

Austin trapped the angry reptile inside the walls of the woven basket by pressing the rim against the floor. He held it down, his heart thumping in his ears, as the two-foot-long snake repeatedly struck.

"Get me something I can put on top, something heavy," Austin said as a relieved sound tore from Maria's throat. There was no way he was going to chance this thing slipping out of its trap.

Maria was next to him in a heartbeat, handing him full bottles of shampoo and conditioner. He piled them on top of the basket, along with a soap dispenser and lotion bottle.

"That should do the trick while I get ahold of animal control." He turned around and his pulse pounded for a different reason. She was standing there, essentially naked, her delicately bronzed skin slick with water from the tub. The fingers on her right hand were white, clutching a towel against her chest, but the thin material fell in a straight line and water dripped from her soft curves.

Austin did his level best to force his gaze away and refocus on the basket, and failed.

She picked up on his actions. Stepping back and wrapping the towel around her, she secured the top edge. He didn't want to notice that her pulse pounded at her throat. Or see the exposed parts that had given them both so much pleasure.

He fished his smartphone out of his front pocket and looked up animal control in Austin. He couldn't help it that his back teeth were clenched so tight he almost couldn't open his mouth to speak. Pretty much all of his muscles corded and his shoulders were so tense he thought his muscles might snap. A large part of that had to do with the snake. And then there was Maria. He missed her from a place he'd shut down when she walked out and for reasons so much more than just her body. Although, having her standing there naked was a sore reminder of…

Austin planted his free hand against the wall.

"I'll just get dressed," Maria said.

"Fine," he bit out a little harsher than he'd expected. *Dammit. Dammit. Dammit.*

Maria returned a few minutes later with her hair pulled up in a ponytail, standing on the other side of the door. She wore pale pink jogging shorts and a similar-colored tank top. He tried not to notice how much the light colors contrasted against her bronzed skin. The necklace he'd given her for their first anniversary was clasped around her neck. She must've forgotten that she'd stopped wearing it last year.

"Someone's on the way from animal control," he said, his voice a little huskier than he'd intended.

"Good." She ran her hands on the outside of her arms with a shiver, keeping her gaze on the basket. "I can't wait for that thing to get out of here."

"We need to call building maintenance and let them know what's going on," he said, forcing his eyes away from her heart-shaped rosy lips. Sexual thoughts were out of line under the circumstances.

"Right," she said, looking like she was trying to mentally shake off the experience. A full-body shiver rocked her as she stood in the doorjamb. "Dave will want to be informed about this, but I'm not leaving until I know that thing is gone."

Austin knew that she wouldn't sleep again until she had searched every inch of the place to make sure there were no others.

"How'd that thing get in here?" Maria was still shaking but tried to cover by rubbing her arms, her nervous tell.

"That's a good question because they aren't from anywhere around here," he stated. Austin knew a lot about snakes thanks to his upbringing on the ranch.

"As in out of Texas or the Southwest?" Maria's voice hitched.

"More like out of this country. I've never seen anything like it in Texas," he said flatly. He pulled up the internet on his phone and input a description. "This one's found in parts of Africa, places in the Middle East, and India."

"Oh." Her mind seemed to be racing, clicking through possibilities. She latched on to the question he'd been asking himself for the past ten minutes. "Why would an exotic snake be in my apartment?"

His first thought was most likely the same as hers based on her knowing expression. He rubbed the scruff on his chin. "I locked the door when I left and opened it with the key when I returned."

"Were there any signs that it had been tampered with?" she asked.

"Nothing that was obvious to me. At least, I thought it was locked. I'm not certain."

Her brow shot up.

Yeah. I know. He was giving away the fact that he wasn't familiar with the loft. All this pretending was for the birds. The only thing he didn't have to fake was his very real attraction and need to protect her. Even after all this time and heartache, that magnetic force still made the earth shift under his boots when she was close.

"There's a chance the door could've already been unlocked and I didn't catch it," he admitted. Austin held his hand up in defense of her reaction. The place was new to him and he'd been carrying a bag of takeout, so he hadn't listened for a click. He'd stuck the key in the lock, turned it a couple of times and walked inside. He hadn't been sure of the direction he needed to twist in order to unlock the door and now he was cursing himself for his carelessness.

"Let's assume it was locked for a minute," she said. "Who else would have a key?"

"Building maintenance, for one, which is obvious." Austin sidestepped the other apparent answer… her fiancé. Surely, the guy wouldn't want to hurt the woman he planned to marry.

He started to make a move for the long table near the door to see if there was a list of neighbors or friends inside a drawer but Maria's reaction stopped him from leaving the bathroom.

"Please stay right there until someone comes to pick that thing up." She motioned toward the basket with a shiver.

He nodded.

"I find it hard to believe that Dave would sneak inside our house and slip a snake inside the bathroom while I was taking a bath."

Austin tensed at the reminder of her being in this room a few minutes ago naked and in the bath.

"What's wrong?" Maria's forehead crinkled in the cutest way when she was concerned.

"It's nothing worth saying out loud." His focus needed to stay on the deadly snake and not drift where it didn't belong, like thoughts of Maria with nothing on.

She shot him a look but he had no intention of explaining.

"We'll canvass the neighbors. See if anyone saw anything," she said.

"What about security cameras? Are there any in the building?" He hadn't thought to check earlier, but then he hadn't needed to know before now.

"Yeah, but I've never had luck with the images from security footage, so I wouldn't be too hopeful. Based on the age of the cameras in the hallway I can already tell it'll be too grainy." Maria had regained her composure as she seemed to switch gears into investigative mode. Her ability to close off her emotions had made her great at doing her job. And now he could see that it had contributed to the undoing of their relationship, too.

Austin was beginning to have doubts that any event in the past week had been random. And that meant talking to her fiancé given that a woman's biggest threat was the people closest to her. He would have access to her apartment. Could he want to harm Maria? Maybe he just wanted to scare her into remembering him.

Austin's mind was going places he didn't like. The list of people who had access to Maria's apartment had two names on it… Dave from maintenance and the fiancé he wasn't supposed to talk about.

A knock at the door came two minutes after the call to Dave ended. Maria checked the peephole before letting him in, confirming it was building maintenance. Austin was keeping an eye on the basket in the next room or he would've been the first one to the door.

"What happened?" Dave asked, sounding concerned as his voice trailed behind Maria. He was in his late thirties and stood at the same five feet seven inches in height as her. He had sandy-blond hair and light eyes. His distress seemed genuine based on the worry lines creasing his forehead.

It could be an act, though, so Austin planned to keep a close watch.

"ANIMAL CONTROL IS on its way." Maria involuntarily shivered just thinking about what had just happened after filling Dave in. The investigator in her had asked him to rush over without giving him a heads-up about what was going on. She'd wanted to gauge his reaction to the news in person. She glanced at the top drawer of her dresser where she kept her service revolver.

"What kind of snake is it?" he asked.

"Viper," she responded.

"What on earth?" he asked, stopping before the bathroom door. He sounded as freaked as she felt. "It's in *there*?"

"Yes," Maria said.

She appreciated the vigilant watch Austin kept on the basket as he introduced himself to Dave. But why the need for introductions? Austin had said that he spent most of his time on the ranch but wouldn't he and Dave already know each other? She'd lived here for a year. Wouldn't they have crossed paths at some point?

Maria made a mental note to ask Austin what that was about later. Right now, she had a deadly snake to get rid of…

"Are you sure it's still in the basket?" Dave asked, dropping down to one knee in the doorway to get eye level with the basket.

Austin nodded and Maria could tell that her husband was sizing up the maintenance man. Austin was huge by comparison. His features darker and his expression far more serious.

"You have any idea why a saw-scaled viper would be in the building?" Austin asked.

A knock at the door sounded before Dave could respond.

"Hold that thought. I'll be right back," Maria said, excusing herself to answer the door. A quick peek through the peephole revealed a man wearing a City of Austin shirt. She let him in.

"Good evening, ma'am." The guy was barely out of his twenties. His hair was already thinning on top and he was a little shorter than Maria. "Name's Mark Tailor and I'm from animal services. We got a call about a snake at your residence."

"Yes," Maria said, opening the door wider. "It's in the bathroom."

She motioned toward the door as another round of heebie-jeebies rocked her. The sooner he got that thing out of her home, the better.

Mark put on a thick set of gloves and made a beeline toward the bathroom. He wore a hunter green shirt with a lighter shade pant. She didn't want to be anywhere near that room when the snake was disturbed. She had no idea if it could run out of venom and had no plans to be anywhere near it to find out.

Austin stood guard at the bathroom door. Dave joined her in the adjacent room.

Mark walked out less than three minutes later with a captured viper making a lot of noise from the bottom of a very thick bag. "This should take care of it."

"Thank you," Maria said as she showed him to the door. She'd breathe easier now that thing was out of her house.

Dave's hands were on his hips when she returned and Austin was moving around, checking behind pillows and pieces of furniture.

"I think I know who that snake belongs to," Dave said.

Maria looked at him expectantly.

"Your downstairs neighbor," he said. "Tyson Greer."

"There's one way to find out if it's his," Austin said, already tracking toward the exit, Dave at his heels.

"If that's the case then I need to have a little chat with this Tyson." Maria wasn't far behind. "And file a complaint. I didn't know tenants were allowed to keep dangerous pets in the building."

Maria knocked on the door a little harder than she'd planned. Her nerves were still heightened so she took a few deep breaths to calm herself. Focusing on treating this incident like an investigation calmed her a few notches. She could easily slip into her role at the FBI and shelve her emotions.

There was no answer.

"I'm calling him right now." Dave's phone was to his ear. "If that was his pet, he'll want to know right away."

Maria knocked again.

Nothing.

The neighbor didn't answer his phone, either. Didn't that get the hairs on the back of her neck to stand up.

"Guess he's not around," Dave said after leaving an urgent message and then ending the call.

"I want to talk to him the minute he responds," Maria said.

"And I have a few of my own questions," Austin stated.

Dave nodded. "I'm sorry this happened. That could've turned out pretty bad."

"It's a good thing I came home when I did." Austin rubbed the scruff on his chin. "Have you checked your key ring?" he asked Dave.

Dave unclipped the set of masters from his belt loop and fanned the couple dozen keys, stopping to account for each one. "They're all here."

Maria's gaze traveled from the keys to his belt loop. She trusted Dave, especially given that the manager had asked her for help with his background check. He'd been clean. She liked Dave and didn't want to look at him as a possible suspect. Experience had taught her not to take anything for granted. People could have a solid background and then end up tempted by the right offer.

Or Dave might've left his keys unattended and someone could've had a copy made.

"Have you had them with you all day?"

Dave brought his index finger up to his lips. His face was a study in concentration as his forehead crinkled. "I don't think so. Let's see. I'm trying to think about where all I've been today."

He ran through a couple of maintenance items that he'd checked off throughout the day, shaking his head as he seemed to mentally check off each one.

"I've been in maintenance for fifteen years and have never seen anything like this," he said.

Maria looked at her husband, studying his reaction. He'd said that he didn't remember if he'd locked the door properly earlier and the look in his eye said that he didn't believe the notion that any of this could be accidental. Maria knew because she was starting to be suspicious, too. But then, a healthy dose of suspicion was a job requirement in her career.

Austin looked at her, that one look more powerful than a confession.

"What is it?" she asked.

"Nothing," he responded.

That look was anything but, she thought.

Dave was going back over his day again. Maria noted that there were several times when he was out in the open and someone could've slipped a key off his ring. A good criminal would know how to make an imprint for a copy or slip the key off and have an extra made before Dave realized it was gone.

She held her hand out toward him. "I'm changing my lock and, at least for now, I'm keeping the only key."

Chapter Five

"Food's getting cold," Austin said to Maria. He'd warmed their meals in the microwave fifteen minutes ago and she'd barely touched hers.

She pushed another bite around the plate with her fork. Her composed expression belied the emotions brimming under the surface, like a volcano under the facade of a calm sea.

He scraped the last bits of his food into the trash, thinking that Denali sure would've enjoyed a few bites of fish taco. "What's wrong?"

"What are the chances what happened earlier is coincidence after being ambushed five days ago?" She looked up at him, that look of defiance beginning to show through in her brown eyes. Her penetrating gaze had always been good at stripping his defenses, so he armored up.

"I'd say slim at best." He set the plate in the sink and then leaned against the counter.

"I need to talk to my downstairs neighbor." She

set her utensil down with a clank, and based on her expression, a little harder than she'd intended.

"Yeah," he said. "I've been listening for him to come home."

"Me, too." She stood and started pacing.

"I doubt we'll hear anything, but just in case," he said, studying her. He'd expected her to be different and yet not much had changed. A piece of him wished they could erase the last year altogether and go back to the place where life was good again. Where he woke tangled in the sheets with her. She'd beam up at him with those big brown eyes when they opened. Austin had believed that he was the luckiest man on earth when she'd said yes to his marriage proposal. The wedding had been a simple affair with just his immediate family. Her mother was already gone and she'd never met her father. With no siblings, it had just been her and there had always been a lone wolf–quality to Maria when he really looked back. He hadn't recognized it at the time and if he had acknowledged it, he would've believed that she'd come around in time.

Quick-witted, Maria had challenged him on every level. Seeing her now looking frustrated and defeated sat hard in his gut. And he needed to have a conversation with her about her fiancé. Not until he spoke to the doctor in charge of her recovery first, he decided.

"I guess I should be grateful that I have something to do now besides sit around and," she glanced around as though searching for the right word, *"...heal."*

She flashed her eyes at him and it was the first real hint of the severity of the blowout that was building inside her, begging for release. He'd seen that look right before all the fight fizzled out of her and she'd walk out the door saying that she needed air.

If he was going to be a help, his personal feelings would need to sit on the back burner.

Besides, he understood her stumbling block. She wasn't the couch potato type. But she needed to slow down and let her wounds get better, not run off half-cocked into a situation that could get her into more trouble. A picture was emerging that he didn't like. Someone had it out for Maria and he had every intention of figuring out who it was.

"It might be best if you take it easy." He motioned toward the couch.

Austin would've thought that he'd just waved a red blanket in front of a bull for the reaction he got.

"I'm grateful for your help, Austin, so don't take this the wrong way. Believe it or not, I can take care of myself." The words came out like a shotgun blast, loud and fragmented.

"Understood." It was probably just rattled nerves that had Maria needing to lash out. When he really thought about it, a reaction from her now was so much better than what he'd gotten before.

"I'm going downstairs," she stated as she stalked toward the door.

He stepped in her path.

"Move out of my way," she said.

"I've been thinking, so hear me out."

He waited for her acknowledgment and continued after she finally nodded. "I don't think it's a good idea for you to go over there like this. We should probably call your boss and let him handle the interview."

Her head was already shaking.

Austin positioned his legs in an athletic stance. She could charge ahead but she was going to meet a wall.

"I have every intention of updating my boss as soon as I figure out if there's anything to report," she said, and he could see based on the fire in her eyes that her fuse would be short.

"You have that out of order." Austin could take whatever she dished out and she probably just needed to blow off steam anyway. He could be her release valve.

"Step aside." She stood toe-to-toe with him now and her jaw was clenched tight.

"Careful," he warned, running his finger along her cheekbone. "You're heading down a thorny path."

When she looked up at him this time, there was a different emotion present in her dark eyes—one they couldn't afford because it made him want things he shouldn't.

Her flat palms pressed against his chest and he could feel her trembling. The strength and calm he saw in her expression was nothing more than a mask that her body couldn't support.

This close, electricity pinged between them. They couldn't afford that, either.

His mind argued that one kiss was all it would take to get her out of his system. Her rosy lips were close enough to claim. All he had to do was dip his head down a little lower.

Instead, he took in a sharp breath to steady his resolve.

And she didn't seem ready to accept defeat.

"You haven't touched me since we came home." She flexed her fingers, smoothing them along his pecs.

"This isn't my home," Austin said. He shouldn't have admitted that to her but holding up the facade was exhausting for an honest man.

"So I noticed. Fine. We belong on the ranch. You won't take me there so I have to ask. Is there someone else?" Those brown eyes stared up at him after a flicker of nervousness.

Wasn't that a stray bullet straight to his heart. "There isn't for me."

"Well then, I don't understand. Don't you want to be with me anymore?" The innocence in her eyes gave way to the heat between them, and became glittery with desire.

And it would be so easy to slip down that path again with Maria.

Austin knew better than to take her mouth but

he didn't resist when she pushed up on her tiptoes and kissed him. At first, she grazed her teeth across his bottom lip before a gentle bite. Then, she gently sucked before he put both his hands around her neck, his fingers curling around the base, and repositioned her so he could claim her mouth. His thumbs rested on her cheekbones as she opened her mouth and he slid his tongue inside.

A firebolt of need scorched through him, the impact cording his muscles.

Her hands wound around his neck, her fingers in his hair and when she pushed up, her breasts were flush against his chest. Her breathing was rapid, like his, and he dropped his arms to circle around her waist. There was so much heat between them as she broke apart first and looked up at him. Her body was rigid, strung tight with the same tension that had had them both climbing to heights he'd never imagined before sex with her, and Austin had always had great sex. With Maria, there were so many more layers to it.

All the emotions mixed up in his head as they slipped into that familiar fire that had consumed them…their hearts pounding in rhythm. Her hands were all over his back now as his dropped to her sweet round bottom. He let out a low growl as her sex ground against him.

Austin lowered his face and kissed her neck. She mewled a sweet, sexy little sound when he hit that spot near the base. Her pulse pounded against his lips and he wanted to pick her up, take her to the bed and claim her one more time as his.

Reality was more effective than a bucket of ice water. Because she wasn't *his*. The two of them didn't belong together anymore and she'd moved on to prove it. As soon as she got her memories back, she'd realize her mistake and push him away again.

He picked her up and took her to the couch, setting her down gently so he didn't hurt any of her injuries. She was most likely expecting a different response than him standing up straight and walking away.

"Austin," she said, winded.

"Yeah."

"What did I do wrong?" she asked.

"Nothing." The word came out in a grunt as he turned to face her.

"I don't mean right this minute," she said. "I'm talking about before."

"Before what?" he asked, his body strung tight with need…need for Maria.

She made that annoyed sound with her tongue. The one she'd gotten so good at right before she walked away from tension leading up to a fight. "You didn't play games with me before. Why do you feel the need to tap-dance around everything now?"

"I have no idea what you're talking about," he said, trying hard to sell it.

Maria sat up straight. "I'm going to remember sooner or later. I'm pretty sure that I just embarrassed myself by coming on to you but I don't recall there ever being a problem between us in the bedroom."

He grumbled out a curse word under his breath.

"So, just tell me what I did. I'd like to apologize," she said.

"There's no need to worry about that," he stated, but she didn't seem to be buying it. "You're not embarrassing yourself."

"You want me, right?" she asked, and there was a vulnerability to her voice that he'd never heard before.

"Yes." He wouldn't deny it.

"And we're married." She hugged a pillow to her chest.

"You already know that we are."

"All I can think about is the great sex we used to have. When we're close, I get the impression you want me, but you pull back." Her cheeks flushed and Austin's heart squeezed at her embarrassment. It wasn't a good idea to let himself get too caught up in the moment. She'd had a near-death experience and wanted proof life was still good. She remembered a few happy times and, lucky her, had blocked out the rest of the hell they'd been through. He could flip an internal switch and have amazing sex with her. It wouldn't take any more encouragement for that. The problem was that sex was more complicated with Maria. There'd be collateral damage and he had no plans to jab a knife through his own heart again. He thought about whether or not he should say anything to her. Not giving her any information seemed cruel. But how much of their past could she handle?

"We've had a few dustups," Austin started.

"Ones that drove this much of a divide between us?" Maria looked up at him, confusion knitting her brows. Her hands came up to rub her temples and she looked like she was trying to stem a raging headache.

"No," he said honestly. It was true. The fight they'd needed to have never came. Instead, they'd grown distant and time had worked against them, creating a gorge so deep that no bridge could connect the sides again. Being apart got easier and easier, especially for her. "I don't think it's a good idea to talk about the past until you're feeling better."

"What really happened to me? Tell me that, at least."

"You were assaulted after leaving a Sixth Street bar with a few coworkers," he supplied. He saw no need to tell her that she was most likely with Mitch.

She sat there and chewed on her lip.

"How am I supposed to move on when I can't remember anything?" she asked, frustration bubbling to the surface now.

"It'll come back," he said.

And when it did, she'd be kicking him out faster than a rat in the food cupboard before running back to the new man in her life.

MARIA COULDN'T GET her arms around her attraction to her husband. It was so much more than a physical connection. As corny as it sounded, even to her, they'd connected on a much deeper level and she could sense the bond even though it felt like she was being met with a wall. He was holding back and he wouldn't clue her in. Given that she remembered in vivid detail just how hot their sex had been—having memorized every strong line of his muscular body—his refusal to make love convinced her that something was really off between them. If only she could remember...

Whatever had happened must've been pretty bad because she saw caution in his eyes. For now, all she could hope was to win his trust enough for him to fill her in on what they'd been going through to cause such a large chasm. There was another thing bugging her. He'd been adamant about not going to the ranch—the only place she remembered as home—which caused her to think the place was somehow connected to their issues. Whatever they could be. One thing was certain—Austin O'Brien had it all, intelligence, sense of humor, on top of being smokin' hot. In lighter moments, she'd seen that they had an easy way with each other and she couldn't for the life of her figure out what could have possibly gone wrong between the two of them.

All couldn't be lost given the fact that he was there, helping her. Even if he was keeping an emotional distance. If she could figure out what was wrong, she could try to fix it and get their lives back on track.

Pain pierced that spot right between her eyes. She needed to give it a rest. Churning over what could've gone wrong was giving her a splitting headache.

Maria made a move to get up and winced.

"I'll get whatever you need. Stay put," Austin said, flat palms toward her.

"Can I have a couple of ibuprofen?" Maria could get her own pain relievers. However, she didn't have the energy to argue so she acquiesced, deciding to pick her battles.

Austin nodded and went to work in the kitchen pouring a glass of water.

There was something else bothering her, like a dark shadow lurking in the background. Maria strained to figure out what but she couldn't reach it for the life of her. She checked her cell and saw that she had a few texts from her coworkers. They must want to know how she was doing. What could she tell them when she remembered so little?

A knock at the door made her jump. But then, she was jumpy.

Austin answered.

"My name is Tyson Greer and I live downstairs," the young male voice said. He sounded nervous and apologetic when he added, "I'm so sorry about what happened."

Maria didn't recognize the voice but that didn't surprise her. She didn't remember living here let alone who her neighbors might be.

Austin let the guy in and motioned for Tyson to

join them in the living room. He brought over the pain relievers, which she immediately took from him. She swallowed both pills with a single gulp of water before introducing herself to Tyson and accepting his handshake.

"Please, sit down." She motioned toward the chair, hoping her head would stop pounding soon.

Tyson perched on the arm of the chair. His face muscles were bunched, there was sweat on his brow and he looked panicked. "I was shocked to hear what happened. Adele has never gotten out of her cage before. I swear it's secure."

Greer had longish curly hair. His light brown locks were tucked into a ponytail. He was in his late twenties, thin and looked like he'd just gotten off tour with a band. That, or worked in advertising as a creative type. His clothes were modern and he had that look that tried to be effortless but was probably a lot of work. He was, however, exactly the kind of person she'd expect to live downtown in a loft. There were plenty of musicians in the city, so that wasn't out of the question, and no shortage of advertising companies he could work for.

"I was working late and had no idea she'd gotten loose," he said, looking anguished. He was twisting his hands together so hard there were red streaks and his face was distorted into a worried frown.

"What do you do?" Maria tried to push up but pain shot through her. She grimaced and blew out a breath.

"Are you okay?" Tyson made a move to help but Austin was already by her side.

"I'm good. Thanks. Got hit coming home from Sixth Street the other night," she said.

"Austin has the worst traffic," Tyson stated.

She nodded, capitalizing on their camaraderie. People gave up more information when they felt comfortable. "Have you lived in Austin your whole life?"

He nodded as more words rushed out. "I completely freaked as soon as I got Dave's message. Like I couldn't believe something like this could happen. I'm so careful with her."

"What about your girlfriend?" she hedged, trying to get a sense of who lived downstairs without coming off as invading his privacy. She could pull her badge and rank but Tyson was already practically shaking and she didn't want him closing up.

"There's no one right now," he said and there was a familiar note to his voice…loneliness?

Maria connected with the emotion but she couldn't pinpoint why it resonated. Then she thought about her relationship with Austin and chalked it up to that.

"Have you had any friends over recently?" she asked.

"Not since my party last weekend but that was just a couple of guys from work coming over to watch the game," he stated.

"Which one was that?" She figured it would be easy to find out if he was lying. Nothing about his body language said he was and her gut agreed. Experience had taught her to fact-check everything involving an investigation. She had to admit, focusing on work made her feel as close to normal as she could be under the circumstances for the first time in days. She could shelve the strange reaction her body had, was still having to her husband and the mixed-up bag of emotions that came as a result.

Tyson glanced up and to the left, a sign he was recalling information.

"Texas-OU," he answered.

"When was the last time you saw the snake in her cage?" she continued.

"This morning when I gave her breakfast," he admitted.

"Dave said you work for the FBI. Am I going to be arrested?" Light blue eyes wide, his youth and innocence had a certain charm.

"No. Nothing like that," she confirmed. "I would like to see where you keep—what's her name?"

"Adele." Relief seemed to wash over him like a tidal wave cleansing sand from a bridge. "Like the singer."

"Mind showing me Adele's cage?" Maria asked, thinking that Tyson seemed genuine enough. She didn't know him personally but his responses to her couple of questions came off as sincere. The job had given her good skills at detecting lies. It was most likely safe to cross this guy off the suspect list. So, it was back to Dave and his keys.

"Not at all," he said, pushing up to his feet.

Austin was already offering a hand up. She took it, ignoring all the confusing kinetics pinging back and forth. The two of them followed Tyson to his place a floor below and Austin's hand rested on the curve of her lower back. It felt so natural there and he seemed genuinely surprised when she stepped away from him. She wasn't trying to be a jerk by putting a little distance between them; she was trying to keep her sanity.

Maria had no idea what a proper snake cage should look like but the one in Tyson's living space looked legit. It wasn't huge. She pointed at what looked to be a light source. "What's this for?"

"Keeps her warm. She's native to Sri Lanka, so she's used to sunshine. I got her after a great surfing vacation there. Guess I wanted something to remind me of the experience. Didn't realize when I got her how long snakes live. It was a stupid decision to keep her and then I didn't feel right getting rid of her. It wasn't her fault that I made a dumb choice, you know." Tyson's place looked like he might be a professional surfer. There were three boards stacked in the corner of the loft and most of his furniture looked recycled. It had an earthy, artistic look, she mused. His layout was similar to Maria's since he was directly below her but it wouldn't have mattered if it wasn't since the whole room was open concept.

"Have you lived here long?" she asked. His place was definitely more settled than hers. There were a few photos hanging of him on various vacations. In one he jumped high in the air over what looked to be a cliff. She'd heard of those as scare-your-momma pics. Another showed him holding on to one of his boards as he stood ankle-deep in clear blue water.

"That one's from South Africa," he said, beaming. "You ever been?"

"Too many deadly sharks for my taste," she said.

"With your line of work, I wouldn't think you'd be afraid of anything," he said.

He had a point.

"I like to face the demons I can see coming," she joked, but there was a strand of truth to it. She preferred monsters on the surface rather than in the deep.

"What will happen to Adele?" Tyson's voice sounded tormented. "I feel like a jerk for letting this happen. I don't know what went wrong. I promise that I always lock her cage."

"I'll see what I can arrange," Austin said as he lifted the lid and tested the lock. That was going to be her next move. He was a natural investigator. "I may be able to get her back to her natural habitat."

"That would be awesome actually." Tyler perked up.

"What about other visitors?" Maria asked. "You mentioned the guys you had over to watch the game. Has anyone been by your place in the past few weeks?"

"Had a guy stop by with his daughter about two

weeks ago. She was selling Girl Scout cookies. I figured they live in the building," Tyson said.

"I don't remember seeing kids here. I'd think that I would've heard one by now," she said.

"He's a weekend-type dad. Shared custody," Tyson stated.

"Did they come inside?" she asked.

"No. Stood at the door," he answered.

"Did you leave them alone at any time?" Maria surveyed the rest of the room.

"Just long enough to get my wallet on the counter." He motioned toward the bar area where there was a pile of mail. He'd pitched his keys there when they'd walked inside.

"So, your back was turned a few seconds," Maria said. "That'd be enough time to get a visual of the place."

Tyson's eyes widened. "I didn't think much about it at the time."

"Anyone else stop by unexpectedly?" She walked over to the stack of mail. It was the usual stuff.

"Those were the only two people." He stared at a spot on the wall, as though trying to remember anyone else. "Yeah, that's it. I'm sure. Work's been busy and I've been doing nothing but working and sleeping."

"No deliveries or maintenance calls?" Maria continued.

Tyson shook his head. "Just work."

By all accounts, this looked like an accident.

Tyson could've been in a rush after a feeding and forgot to lock the cage. Mistakes happened.

Austin tested the lock on the snake's cage one more time. "Everything's in good working order."

"I'm mega careful," Tyson said, hands on his head, looking exacerbated. "I'd be crazy not to take every precaution with her. She's deadly and I didn't give that nearly enough respect when I got her. I wasn't thinking about how long the commitment would be or the fact that she might figure a way out of her cage one day."

It might've been Maria's imagination but she could swear that she saw Austin nodding out of the corner of her eye.

"I'm just so glad that nothing happened other than a scare," Tyson said, and his face paled. "I mean, I'm not taking this lightly but this could've been so much worse, right?"

"It could've," Maria agreed. She didn't want to acknowledge just how close she'd come to being bitten. Her body shivered at the thought.

"Are we cool after this?" Tyson asked. He was so nervous that his hands were shaking and her sense was that he was a good guy. She could easily verify whether or not he'd been working as much as he said, but she suspected he was. There was no drug paraphernalia in his apartment or warning signs that he could be something more than he was projecting.

"Sure." She offered a smile.

"There's nothing else to be done here," Austin said to Maria.

How much of their current relationship did that statement cover?

Chapter Six

Austin stretched out sore legs. Sleeping on the couch, if he could call it sleep, for the past few nights had caused him to rack up some seriously angry muscles. He needed a cup of strong black coffee.

A hint of light peeked through the wall of windows. The sun would rise above the buildings soon. As it was there was barely enough light in the kitchen to move around easily.

"That smells amazing," Maria said from the open-concept bedroom. He didn't want to remember being so close that he could hear her breathe last night.

"I was just about to pour a cup." He pulled two mugs out of the dishwasher. "How's your head this morning?"

"A couple of ibuprofen and a cup of coffee will go a long way toward making me feel human again." She threw off the covers but was slow to her feet.

"Doc wants something in your stomach before you take those." Austin set two pills next to a piece of fruit and yogurt—her favorites—on the place mat of the breakfast bar. He added a glass of water to the mix.

Maria did the same thing he would've done, grabbed the coffee mug first. He cracked a smile.

"What?" she asked, crooking her head to one side.

He didn't want to think how beautiful she was in the morning, or how much her sleepy grin tugged at his heart. That road would lead nowhere fast. Unless misery was a town he wanted to revisit. No, thanks.

"Nothing. I woke up thinking about your assault last week and then what happened last night." He sipped the dark liquid to clear the haze from his mind, a haze that had him noticing the flush to Maria's cheeks that she always had in the early-morning hours.

"The timing has been bothering me, too." She finished her fruit and yogurt before palming the ibuprofen and tossing them into the back of her throat.

Austin forced his gaze away from the soft lines of her neck as she threw her head back.

"I'll be good as new by—" she glanced at the clock on the microwave "—six twenty."

She pinched the bridge of her nose, her I'm-about-to-get-a-raging-headache move. The rest of her body language said that was an overstatement, which was not surprising given recent events. Her back was rigid and she clenched her fingers around the coffee mug. Since a round of tension-breaking sex was out of the question, he figured that she needed some semblance of her old routine back. The added benefit was that she might remember something from her past. It had occurred to him last night as he lay awake staring out the window that the reason for these incidences might very well be locked in her memories.

Trying to think seemed to make his head hurt.

He walked over and then picked up the pair of running shoes docked next to the door. "We're going for a jog today."

"We are?" Her face lit up.

"I know how much you like it and I figured you could handle getting outside." He dangled the pair of shoes. "You have to swear you won't push yourself, though. Doc hasn't technically cleared you for exercise."

"I'll walk if it means getting out of this place in the fresh air." She lunged toward him and snatched the shoes out of his hands. "Ha. You can't stop me now, mister."

He wouldn't share the part where he'd let her beat him. It was worth it to see her keep her smile.

She was already tying her laces when he said, "We should check in with your boss this morning. Let him know about yesterday."

"I was just thinking the same thing." She popped her head up and locked gazes for half a second.

It was enough to make Austin's body react in more ways he didn't want to acknowledge.

A red blush crawled up Maria's neck as she looked away. "You must have something besides boots around here. Hold on—"

"I don't," he said before she could get too far down that path. "My running shoes are in my truck."

"Oh." A curious look darkened her features. "Okay."

"We'll grab 'em on the way out." Getting her moving would hopefully stem the flow of questions building behind her eyes.

She followed him to the elevator and down and to his truck before the first one came out. "Why don't you have any shoes at my place?"

He started to answer. Then it seemed to dawn on her.

"We weren't in a 'little dustup,' were we?" she asked.

"No." Austin opened the driver's-side door, and then grabbed his spare pair of runners off the back floorboard.

He shut the door.

"Ready?" he asked.

She paused, bit her bottom lip, and then nodded.

Two minutes later, they were on the Lady Bird Lake Hike-and-Bike Trail. Austin waited while Maria stretched.

"We'll take it slow at first and then build to a comfortable pace," Austin said, trying to steer the conversation back on track before she shot off another question he didn't want to answer.

"Sounds like a plan."

Austin folded his arms and looked out over the lake as she alternated rolling her ankles.

"Any chance we can go kayaking this afternoon?" she asked.

Austin thought about the first time they'd visited the capital together and done that very thing. They'd found a quiet cove while the sun set, she'd straddled him and they'd made love right there on Barton Creek. He was pretty sure that she wasn't referring to that.

"Let's see how you feel after lunch. Time to get the blood moving," he said, taking a couple of strides.

Maria caught up and then fell in step next to him.

This early, there were only a few dedicated joggers on the path. The capital was beautiful in the early-morning hours. Normally, the whole city was too crowded for Austin's taste but there was a quiet calm now that made him feel connected to the city with his namesake, a feeling similar to the ranch.

"Mind if we pick up the pace?" Maria asked with a glance toward him.

"Not at all." Austin increased his speed to a light jog.

"You can do better than that," Maria teased before taking off in a fast run.

She made it two blocks before she dropped to her knees under the bridge and gripped her head with both hands, rocking back and forth. "Blood is pounding."

Austin looked around for something…anything… a water fountain or a place to lie down. Didn't see either. He located a bench and figured that would be better than gravel.

In one smooth motion, Austin helped her to her feet and walked her to the park bench.

"It'll settle down in a minute," he said, stroking her hand.

Her eyes were shut but she hadn't stopped the rocking motion.

It took a full five minutes for her to regain her composure.

"I'm better," she said, making a move to get up. Her expression belied her words but he gave her credit for pushing past the pain. She'd always had a remarkable ability to do that, to shut out everything else and develop a singular focus. He'd assumed that concentration was how she'd survived losing her mother in a brutal death during Maria's tender teenage years. Austin couldn't imagine navigating his hormonal teen years without his parents. Now that he'd lost his to murder, he had an inkling of the pain Maria must've felt.

They'd been walking a good five minutes when Austin heard whimpering noises from the brush to the right. He glanced around. He'd heard similar noises on the ranch. An animal was in trouble.

"Do you hear that?" Maria asked, already tracking toward the sound.

And then Austin saw something move out of the corner of his eye. He glanced around and didn't see anyone else on the path.

A chill gripped his spine. An animal. Hurt. While the two of them were alone on a trail.

Was another "coincidence" about to happen?

"Stay low," he said to Maria, who seemed to catch on to the warning issued in his tone.

She kept her back to him and toward the trail while pulling out her service revolver. He recognized it immediately, the gun she'd nicknamed Shelby.

"You're okay, boy," Austin soothed the frightened animal. There was nothing about this situation he liked as he bent down to scoop the wounded mutt into his arms. He'd always had a gentle hand with livestock and this little guy seemed to realize that he was there to help.

The brown-and-white cocker spaniel mix cried as Austin picked it up, so he immediately set it down and dropped to his knees beside it.

"Is he okay?" Maria asked.

Austin examined the pup. He hadn't grown into his paws so he couldn't be a year old yet. There was a deep cut on his back leg. The gash was too clean to be an accident. Austin surveyed the area and saw a piece of broken glass with blood on it that looked like it had been hastily discarded in the brush.

"Some jerk did this to him," Austin said.

Maria tensed but her gaze continued to sweep the pathway, indicating that she knew exactly what the implication was.

Austin carefully embraced the animal in the same

way he would a calf in a ditch, with his arms around the body.

"Let's get off the trail and take sidewalks from here." There'd be more foot traffic on the upper level since they were nearing the morning rush-hour crush. That window of time lasted two and a half hours. Roads would clog even more as commuters packed the lanes leading into downtown. The capital's traffic was never good and yet another reason Austin couldn't often connect to the city that shared his name.

On the walk back, he'd expected an ambush. Maria wasn't in the best shape but her adrenaline seemed to kick in, giving her an extra push to make the walk home. Relief was a thick blanket on a cold night when they made it to her building without incident.

Inside, Austin gently placed the animal on the sofa. He made a call, dropped his name and a vet arrived fifteen minutes later.

"Come on in," Austin said to the vet who'd introduced herself as Dr. Hannah.

"I see that he isn't wearing a collar," Dr. Hannah, a petite blonde, said as she examined the animal.

"That's just the way we found him," Austin answered.

The vet touched his ribs. "He's young but he's too thin. If he belongs to someone they aren't taking very good care of him."

"If he got out of his yard someone might be looking for him," Austin reasoned.

"He could've been wandering around for days or weeks. We need to make sure information gets posted about him to see if we can locate his owner," the vet said.

"In the meantime, he can come home to my family ranch to heal," Austin said, moving aside to give the vet plenty of space to work. Maria had gone noticeably silent and Austin worried that she'd done herself more harm than good with the walk.

The vet finished patching up the little dog's leg. "I have a feeling that this guy's life just improved more than he'll ever know."

"Once I make sure he doesn't belong to a local family, we'll make a permanent place for him," Austin said. "We'll take good care of him, Doc."

The vet smiled up at him and Maria stepped in between their line of sight, essentially blocking Dr. Hannah's view. What was that all about? Jealousy? Austin wouldn't touch that irony with a ten-foot pole.

"His leg will be okay, right?" Maria asked the vet.

Austin walked into the kitchen to make a cup of coffee. He called his older brother, Dallas, and filled him in on what had happened with the dog.

"I can head that way now to pick up the little guy if you want," Dallas said.

"That would be great if you can get away," Austin replied. "How are the calves?"

"The same," Dallas stated.

"At least it's not worse." Austin took a sip of coffee.

"True." Dallas paused. "How are you, by the way?"

"Never better," Austin said. O'Brien brothers weren't exactly known for asking for help or talking about their troubles. Having each other, knowing any one of his brothers would be there in a heartbeat if he asked, was all the support he needed.

"All right." Dallas wouldn't need a lengthy explanation. He'd pick up on Austin's mood based on his tone. And right now, he was pretty sure that Dallas would hear the internal battle he had going on loud and clear.

"You're doing a good thing," Dallas said. There was something present in his voice that Austin couldn't put his finger on and he worried that his brother was shielding him from the situation on the ranch.

"The calves are stable, right?"

"Yeah," Dallas reassured.

"Okay." He didn't exactly feel better but he was most likely reading too much into his brother's voice.

"Have any memories surfaced?" Dallas asked.

Austin turned to look at Maria who was hovering over the small animal. "Nothing yet."

"They'll come back," Dallas offered.

That's what Austin was afraid of. He reminded himself, again, not to get too comfortable with the new alliance he and Maria had built. It would be all too easy to slip back into old habits with her. And where would that leave him?

"Hey, Ivy League," Dallas began, "you sure you're all right? No one would blame you for handing this situation off."

"I can handle it." By the time Austin finished his call the vet was done with her exam and had treated the spaniel mix.

"I think you've found a good home," Dr. Hannah said to the pup before standing. She smiled at Austin and that seemed to add insult to injury to Maria who seemed ready to boil over.

Austin decided to step in.

"Thank you for coming on such short notice," he said, angling toward the door. "Janis will take care of the invoice."

The blonde nodded, beaming up at him.

Maria sat next to the dog and said quiet words meant to soothe him. She'd always had a way with animals and he remembered how much Denali, the family's Lab, had missed her when she left. He'd stop in to see her and seemed genuinely confused by her disappearance. He'd waited on the porch several Friday nights, the night she'd always come home.

In the hard days following the miscarriage she'd sit outside, rubbing his ears for hours before crossing the threshold. Austin could kick himself now for letting her. He should've walked outside and taken her into his arms instead of not knowing what to do and not wanting to make it worse. He should've done something to let her know that he still cared. He'd been an idiot. And it had cost him their relationship. He could own up to his mistakes even if they weren't fixable now.

Austin walked Dr. Hannah out and then thanked her again.

"We need to talk to your boss and update him on what's been going on," he said to Maria after closing the door.

Maria eyed him carefully as he poured another cup of coffee. "You don't think this was a coincidence, do you?"

"No. I think we were being set up," he said, remembering the prickly feeling he'd had, the way his neck hairs had stood on end. The gut instinct he'd had that someone was watching.

"For another 'accident'?" she asked.

"Could've been a fishing expedition to see what kind of protection you had," he said and then held up a mug. "Do you want another?"

"I can get it on my own," she said, and he could sense that a wall had come up between them.

Had a memory stirred?

Austin braced himself as she breezed past him. He wanted to tell her that she didn't have to get up... that she could—oh, hell. He fisted his hand and bit his tongue. Maria was a strong woman and her mind was made up.

"I'll call my supervisor," she said after pouring a cup.

They stood in the kitchen for a silent moment and he had no idea what was going on inside her mind.

MARIA DIDN'T HAVE the first idea what to say to Austin about the vet flirting with him. He hadn't reciprocated and yet the whole scenario still felt like a slap in the face. Estranged or not they were still married. Did the woman not see that Austin's wife was in the room? People could be so rude.

The conversation going on inside her head distracted her from doing what she'd said she was going to do and netted a curious look from Austin.

She located her cell and dialed Special Agent in Charge Vickery's number.

He picked up just before the call rolled into voice mail.

"Maria, what's up?" His tone was casual but to the point. There was something else she couldn't quite put her finger on. She shelved the thought for now.

"Vic, we need to talk—"

"I already said that you need a doctor's clearance to come back to work," he said impatiently, like he'd been expecting that argument.

"I'm not trying to suit up." Although, she could access her work files from home. She needed to update her boss on what was going on, and she needed to look over the last cases she was working on before the first accident. Austin was right. This was a little too coincidental for her taste. Besides, putting her investigator hat on was like slipping into an overcoat, worn and comfortable. After witnessing firsthand the vet's flirtation with her husband, she felt more at ease thinking about work than addressing her emotions. And that had seriously ticked her off.

She heard a noise, like an impatient cluck come through the line. Vic. Right.

"Sorry. Lost my train of thought for a second. I need to update you on some stuff that's been going on since being released from the hospital," she said.

"Oh…okay…tell me what's happening." There was so much hesitation in Vic's voice. What was up with that? "You're coming back, right?"

"Yeah, of course," she said. Why did he sound so…*weird*? Or maybe *awkward* was a better word. "Some strange stuff has been happening that I want to run past you."

"Like what?" Now he sounded concerned. Now he sounded like Vic.

She filled him in on the snake and the walk on Lady Bird Trail near Zilker Park.

"It's not like anyone's coming straight at me and it could be coincidence, but I thought you should know," she said.

"I'm glad you told me. I agree with you. This is suspicious," Vic said after a thoughtful pause.

"It might be good if I come into the office and take a look at my files. Maybe something will spark and I can tie this up in a bow before something worse happens," she said.

"Under no circumstances are you to come into work," Vic said. "I'll be hauled in front of Internal Affairs if I let you walk through the door without explicit doctor's orders. You're on leave and you can't have anything to do with this place."

Right. *That.* Maria understood why he'd say that when she really thought about it. Okay, fine, she'd access her work via her laptop. She still had credentials, so she'd pull up her files from home.

"Tell me you won't show up at the office and get me in trouble," Vic said, sounding like he needed a cold beer. At least he finally came across as normal, she mused. "This new information needs to be added to the investigation."

"Don't worry. I won't do anything rash," she said.

"I'll send someone over to get a statement from you," he added. "In the meantime, do me a favor and rest, heal so you can get back to work."

"Will do, Vic." She knew exactly what she needed to do and she didn't need her boss's permission.

"I don't like any of what you told me so far, Maria," Vic said. "In fact, I'm putting a protective detail on you until I absolutely know you're safe or we put someone behind bars."

"We don't have the resources," she countered, hating the thought of taking someone off their caseload to babysit her. Not to mention the fact that she already had an overprotective husband and she was pretty certain this event had rocketed his instincts into high gear. "I'll be more careful in the future."

"Yes, you will. And you'll start with accepting the company I'm sending." The crinkling noise of Vic unwrapping a Hershey's bar came through the phone.

Every time he came across an especially stressful or high-profile case, he opened one of those candy bars, broke off a piece and tossed it in his mouth. With that ritual came a commitment to solve the case before the last piece of chocolate was gone. If he couldn't resolve it, the wrapper stayed on his desk. In twenty-plus years at the FBI, there were exactly three wrappers with one piece of chocolate still in them. He'd lined them up on the edge of his desk so he would never forget how much it stung to let a hardened criminal walk free on the streets.

Vic unwrapping chocolate was a bad sign. And she couldn't argue his logic.

"Okay. You're right. I accept," she said.

"Good." There was a pause like he expected her to put up more of a fight.

She didn't. Not taking this threat seriously could cost a life, hers or Austin's. No way would she take that risk.

"I'll get an agent on it." Vic sounded relieved.

Maria thanked her boss before ending the call. The department couldn't afford to lose an agent like her, either. Plus, catching whoever was after her would keep a dangerous person off the streets. The unsub, or unknown subject, had done something worth covering up.

And she intended to figure out what.

Chapter Seven

Austin stood there, leaning his hip against the kitchen counter. He had a coffee mug in his hand and his gaze focused on her.

"Vic's sending over a babysitter," she said.

"That's probably a good idea," he stated. The air had changed and he seemed to realize from this moment on there was a ticking clock. Someone wanted to get to Maria. "Whoever is behind this is trying to make it look like an accident."

"Which could mean that he has a lot to lose if he's discovered. More so than just his freedom. This might involve preserving reputation and standing," she said, grateful for the distraction. Focusing on her case gave her a much-needed break from rehashing where their relationship had gone wrong…and it had gone wrong. She didn't care what her handsome rancher husband said. There was so much he wasn't telling her. She still felt chemistry burning between them but his face told a different story. His eyes said they had serious problems.

Digging in to work was probably for the best. Austin didn't seem ready to talk and she desperately needed another focus.

"He could be a high-profile person," he said. "Someone with a lot to lose in the community if word gets out about his actions."

"His reputation would be ruined," she said, nodding agreement.

"Can we look at what you were working on before your attack?" Austin took a sip and some of the dark liquid remained on his bottom lip when he set the cup down.

Maria focused on retrieving her laptop. "I don't remember much about my recent caseload. I've been racking my brain. All I have as a result so far is a headache."

He shot her a look that sent electricity skittering across her skin. It was a knowing look and she was pretty certain that there wasn't any sexual intent behind it and yet her arms goose bumped anyway. Austin O'Brien had always had that effect on her. The two of them had always had the kind of off-the-charts chemistry that she'd never experienced with another man.

Maria refocused, shutting down those feelings and putting up a wall.

"What is it?" he asked.

She stared at him blankly.

"I can tell something's wrong," he said.

She shrugged. "I can't pinpoint it."

"I thought maybe you remembered something," he said as something dark passed behind his eyes.

"I wish. Maybe digging in to work will stimulate something." Her fingers danced on the keyboard as she refocused her attention.

"Maria," he said, and his voice was low.

"Yeah." She didn't look up.

"Just remember one thing, will you?" There was a quiet-calm quality to his voice now and it washed over her.

"Promise," she said.

"No matter what else happens, know that I loved you the best I could." His voice was heavy as he turned and then walked out the door.

Didn't that send a chill racing up her back that frosted any warmth still there from earlier. Should she ask her husband to explain what he meant by that? Maybe it would connect the scrambled pieces in her mind and she'd find some peace with the past. As it was, she felt like she was walking defenseless down an unlit street with a dark force trailing behind in the shadows.

Maria had no idea how to process what he'd said. Had she done something before to hurt him? If she couldn't remember, how could they make it right? She got a brain cramp thinking about it. The doctor had warned against trying to force her memories to come back. There was so much she wanted to know but couldn't ask. Should she go after Austin and demand that he tell her what was going on?

A dark, helpless feeling came over her, connecting her to a deep and mournful pain. There were no memories along with the ache, just an intensely sad emotion pervading her thoughts.

Her mind flashed to her childhood, to the past, to her mother. That same helpless feeling washed over her. She remembered the argument they'd had the morning her mother had been killed. Maria recalled saying angry words before rushing out the door for school. Halfway there, she remembered leaving the door unlocked. She'd returned, using that as an excuse, but all she really wanted to do was hug her mom and apologize.

Then there was the overwhelmingly bad feeling she'd had when she walked up to their apartment and saw the half-opened front door, the trail of red leading to the kitchen where her mother lay in a pool of blood, lifeless.

It had been Maria's fault for not locking the door. She'd let the killer in and he'd gotten away with murder. There'd been no justice and certainly no mercy. After the initial pain eased, all Maria could focus on was getting her day in court. She'd wanted to face that monster who'd destroyed her family.

Weeks passed and then months with no leads. The detective on the case seemed to lose hope of finding the murderer. And, with it, interest. Maria never got the answers she so desperately needed. Without them, there'd been no closure, no way to move on.

Taking a deep breath, Maria entered her username and password into the prompt after pulling up the FBI's intranet. Giving justice to others was the best way to keep the past from consuming her. She couldn't change what had already happened but she could find out why someone seemed hell-bent on hunting her.

A message flashed across the screen. Access denied?

Maria cursed as she entered her credentials for the third time and was still locked out of the system. Her cell phone rang but she didn't have to answer to know who was calling. That would be Vic. He'd most likely asked IT to alert him if she tried to log on from home.

Dammit. Dammit. Dammit.

There had to be something she could do to access her work files…or her memory. Frustration ate at her as she retrieved her cell and scrolled through the contacts, hoping to jar something loose in her infuriating brain.

Her finger hovered over the list. She stopped on a name.

Mitch DeCarlo… *Mitch DeCarlo?*

The name rang a bell. She racked her brain trying to figure out how she knew him. Mitch DeCarlo.

Nothing.

Why did he sound so familiar? Would Austin know?

"IT'S REALLY GOOD to see you, man," Austin greeted his brother the second the driver's-side door of his pickup truck opened.

Austin needed to be able to talk to someone honestly more than he needed to breathe. Every time he looked at his wife he could see the questions mounting in her eyes and he wanted to give answers, not dance around the topic. He couldn't without risking her health and he wouldn't do that no matter how much he needed to say what was on his mind. Being with her brought up too many feelings best buried. They weren't making any progress. Every time they got close, a wall came up and they stopped talking. They were the same people, making the same mistakes.

"Glad I could be here," Dallas said after a bear hug. He motioned toward the top of the building. "How's it going up there?"

"I'm stuck in between doing what's right for her and setting the record straight," Austin said honestly. There was something about his brother's demeanor that gave him pause.

"Meaning she still doesn't remember anything and you're doing what's best for her instead of what's right for you." Dallas shook his head slowly in a sign of empathy.

"No, she doesn't." He left the other part of the statement alone because his brother would do the same thing and they both knew it. "Did Tommy mention anything to you about what he learned from Deputy Garretson?"

"No, why?" Dallas's eyebrow severely arched and

Austin realized that his brother assumed he was talking about their parents' murder investigation.

"It's about Maria," he clarified. "She's planning her wedding to someone else."

Dallas looked as though he'd taken a physical punch. It was the same way Austin had felt when he'd heard the news.

"Sorry to hear that," his brother said. "I knew you two had been having trouble but I never imagined it would come to this. Can't be easy to pretend like nothing's wrong when you've been hit with that curveball."

"Her biggest surprise is that I brought her here. She believes that she still lives at the ranch," he stated.

Dallas muttered a curse. It was in line with the one Austin was thinking.

"I can't imagine what it must be like. You're one helluva man for putting her needs first under the circumstances, Austin."

He knew that his brother would've done the same thing if the roles were reversed but he appreciated Dallas for saying so.

"Any other calves getting sick?" Austin asked, needing to think about something else besides the problems he was having with Maria.

"Two more were sent to the quarantine pen," Dallas said, catching on and leaving the topic alone. "Vet's still baffled. The earlier ones are losing weight."

"That's not a good sign. Let's hope it's just a virus

and nothing more serious," Austin said. "Keep me in the loop." He'd been so caught up in Maria's situation that he hadn't thought about how much he was letting everyone down back home. "I have a lot of paperwork to fill out. Do you need me—"

Dallas put up a hand to stop him before he could even finish his sentence. "You take care of what you need to and let us worry about what's going on in Bluff. The ranch will be fine until you're ready to come back."

"That's fair." Austin glanced at the door. "You want to head up and get a cup of coffee?"

Dallas nodded, the ominous look returning. "If you're ready. I'm here if you want to talk."

"Then, let's head up," Austin said, brushing past the offer. He'd already said more than he'd planned but his brother needed to know so he didn't bust the ruse. "She has a stalker and it'll be best if we talk about it with her."

Dallas followed Austin inside the building.

Maria glanced up from the laptop as soon as the door opened and Austin walked inside the apartment. An awkward look passed between her and Austin before she settled her gaze on Dallas.

"It's so good to see you, Dallas," she said, breaking into a wide smile. Her eyes were red rimmed and Austin could've sworn she sniffed back a tear. But then emotions were hard to read on Maria. She wasn't the type to wear them on her sleeve. After what she'd gone through in her teenage years, he could understand why she'd need to feel in control at all times. He couldn't help but think it also made it difficult to be in a relationship with her. Not that she'd been the only one to blame. He'd fallen short as a husband. Life hadn't taught him how to deal with losing a baby and he hadn't been the man Maria needed. But then she'd been the one to walk away without so much as an angry word or a chance to fight for their relationship.

"Same here," Dallas said before walking over and giving her a hug.

"How's everything at the ranch?" she asked, and she must've been picking up on Dallas's tension based on the way her gaze fixed on him.

"I'll get that cup of coffee," Austin said to Dallas, figuring he'd leave the two of them to get reacquainted. Maria accepted his offer of refilling hers.

"Is this the little guy?" Dallas asked, walking over to the couch and zeroing in on the spaniel mix.

"Guess he needs a temporary name," Maria said. "Any ideas?"

A look passed behind Dallas's eyes as Austin handed him the drink. After setting Maria's on the table, he turned to his brother and asked, "What's wrong?"

Dallas motioned for everyone to sit.

They did and Austin's gut clenched. Whatever was going on wasn't good.

"It's Denali," he started and then stopped long enough to shake his head. He didn't seem able to make eye contact with Austin and that wasn't a good sign, either.

"What happened?" Austin asked. "Is he okay?"

"We called the vet the second we found him in the laundry room. Dr. Peters is by his side," Dallas continued. His gaze seemed intent on the patch of wood floor at his feet. "Far as we can tell, he's been poisoned."

Maria gasped. "Oh, no. Will he—" She didn't seem able to finish her sentence.

"Peters won't give the odds of him pulling through. He's letting us spend as much time with him as we want," Dallas said, shooting a look that twisted Austin's gut. "I didn't want to deliver the news over the phone and I know how hard it is for you to go home right now. We're keeping vigil and we'll keep you posted on any new developments. He's critical but stable for now."

The words bounced around Austin's head but he had a hard time letting them in. There was no way he could lose Denali, his loyal friend. Austin had already lost so much—Maria's pregnancy, Maria and then his parents. Raw, angry emotions pushed to the surface. Austin had to work to keep them at bay. Because he also realized the implication. His parents had been poisoned. Whoever did this to Denali was familiar and had access to the ranch.

"Where was he?" Austin asked.

"In the main house, the hallway off the kitchen that goes into the laundry room," Dallas supplied.

"That makes me think he might've been about to expose someone's presence," Austin stated, rubbing the scruff on his chin. It had been a few days since he'd shaved and his thoughts hadn't been on the ranch lately. He'd been too busy focusing on his wife. *Almost ex-wife* a voice in the back of his head reminded. It was an important cue and one he needed to remember because he could feel himself starting to drown.

"I'm so sorry," Maria said. And then she gasped and cupped her hand over her mouth. "Ohmygosh, I remember reading about your parents in the newspaper. But why would I read about it? Why wouldn't I be there personally? I mean, we were married at the time, weren't we?"

Austin and Dallas exchanged glances before breaking eye contact and staring at the floor.

"A lot has gone on in the past year, Maria," Austin said. "We should talk about it later."

She seemed thoroughly confused and Austin felt bad. He thought about the man she shared her secrets with now. It wasn't Austin anymore. Thinking about the other guy and the divorce papers sitting on his desk went a long way toward easing Austin's guilt and bringing the rage he'd been burying to the surface.

"Is it safe at the ranch?" he asked Dallas because the admission meant that his parents' murderer was still around.

"We're taking every precaution to make sure,"

Dallas said. "We've cut the staff down to essential employees only to safeguard them and keep them off property for now. We sent them on their way with laptops so they can work from home. Fisher has everything on lockdown."

Gideon Fisher was head of security at the ranch. "I'm guessing that means he didn't get anyone on camera."

"Whoever it was knew the blind spots in the system," Dallas supplied. "There was a boot print and I already know what you're going to ask. A deputy paid a visit to Uncle Ezra's with a warrant. They didn't find a match."

"Doesn't mean he didn't own one," Austin stated under his breath. Their uncle had been hauled in a couple of times for questioning but his ironclad alibi held. He'd been at Aunt Bea's house the entire night of the murders, hassling her about trying to get more of her shares of the ranch.

"Is there any chance you can set that aside for now? I see that the two of you have a lot on your plates already," Dallas said.

Austin started to argue but held his tongue. He was making sense whereas Austin wanted to point a finger. If there was a crack in Uncle Ezra's story, Tommy would bust it wide-open soon enough. Austin clenched and released his fists. Instead of heading down an unproductive path, he told Dallas about the snake and then the incident in the park.

"I'm locked out of the system," Maria added, throwing her hands up in the air.

"Do any of your recent work projects stand out in your mind?" Dallas asked after taking a minute to contemplate everything he'd been told.

"None that I can think of," Maria said. "There's always a degree of danger to my job but I can't think of anyone who'd want to outright hurt me because of a case. But then I don't remember much of anything in the past year right now. I still can't believe that I forgot about your parents. I'm so sorry."

"We probably should've seen that coming," Austin said, referring to being locked out and because he couldn't go there with her right now. Yes, he'd needed her when his parents had been murdered. She'd called but he'd been too stubborn to answer. Part of him *still* needed her. But he'd survived the past year and he'd figure out a way to do the same until the walls stopped closing in around him when he thought about her and his chest didn't cave in at the mention of her name.

"The FBI wouldn't want you to have access while out on medical leave in case you got the bright idea to work," he said.

"I work in the Crimes Against Children program," she said to Dallas, nodding to acknowledge Austin's comment about the lockout. "So, I would imagine there are a lot of people who aren't thrilled with me. I mean, people who masqueraded as family friends or community leaders whose intent was to hurt children generally have a lot to lose. But I can't remember anything specific about my recent caseload."

"What about coworkers?" Austin asked.

"I thought about that. I can't talk to them without asking them to violate policy and I don't want to put them in that position because my friends would do it even if it was bad for their careers."

"That's understandable," Austin conceded, wondering just who her friends were now that she'd gotten the promotion she'd wanted. She hadn't really talked about having friends at work before so mentioning them now struck him as odd.

Maria stroked the young dog's fur. His eyes were closed and he looked mighty comfortable curled up on the couch beside her. "Which reminds me, do you know Mitch DeCarlo?"

Chapter Eight

Austin stood up and moved to the sink as his tendons tightened to the point he thought they might snap. He knew exactly who DeCarlo was but he had no plans to discuss the man with Maria. They'd need to deal with the name at some point and she'd remember that he was the man she loved now. Austin didn't want to imagine that she looked at DeCarlo with the same eyes with which she'd once looked at him. Between that and the news about Denali, Austin's muscles corded tighter. They were already wound up like a spring, ready to launch at any second with the right release mechanism and there would be collateral damage.

"I've never met him," he said, gritting his back teeth.

Dallas seemed to take the cue because he got to his feet quickly and scooped the dog in his arms gently. "I need to head back to the ranch."

Maria walked Dallas to the door.

"Call when you get more news about Denali,"

Austin said to his brother. There was so much swirling around in his head right now as anger roared through him. His parents' murderer was loose. Denali was with the vet, his life hanging in the balance. And that was on top of everything going on with Maria and the lies he was being forced to tell her.

Austin took in a sharp breath. He hated deceiving her.

She looked exhausted and he was relieved when she wanted to curl up on the couch and watch a movie for the rest of the afternoon.

Halfway in, she fell asleep.

A midday knock at the door caused her to stir, but she didn't wake.

Austin had settled in at the breakfast bar with a fresh cup of coffee and the newspaper. He opened the door and introduced himself to the agent.

"My name's Special Agent Cliff Ford, but you can call me Cliff," he said as he shook Austin's outstretched hand. The guy looked to be in his early thirties, close to Austin's age. He was about five foot nine and built like he maintained a military-precise workout regimen. He was dressed in jeans and a T-shirt and would fit easily into the Austin crowd were it not for his crisp haircut, which gave him that law enforcement look.

A knot formed in Austin's gut from thinking that this guy might be friends with DeCarlo. He already knew from Tommy that it was a small world. "Did your boss brief you on the…*situation* with Maria?"

"He did," Cliff said. "Said not to bring up anything about the past and to tell her that he isn't exactly thrilled that she tried to get into the database."

"Is she in trouble for that?" Austin asked.

"Nah, Vic will get over it," Cliff said with a casual smile before motioning toward his head. "Her personal life's been wiped out, too?"

It was more question than statement, so Austin nodded.

"Still thinks we're married," he whispered.

"I thought you were," Cliff said, a look of surprise crossing behind his light eyes.

"What?" Maria told everyone they were still married? He had divorce papers on his desk to prove that she wanted something else. He sure as hell hadn't been the one to initiate the paperwork. And then there was the inconvenient issue of Mitch DeCarlo.

But then Maria had always played her cards close to her chest. Maybe he should tell her to call the guy and see if talking to him stirred any memories. It might make life easier for all involved if she remembered something.

"You want to come inside?" Austin asked, opening the door wider.

"No, thanks. I figure I'll walk the perimeter. Keep an eye on things from out here for a while," Cliff said. "We should stay in touch, though."

"Here's my cell." Austin rattled off the numbers.

Cliff entered the digits in his phone and then provided his. "It goes without saying but if you two go anywhere, you let me know first. Feel free to text or call anytime."

"Same here," Austin said. "You see anything you don't like, let me know."

"There's nothing I like about an agent being stalked. People who mess with law enforcement have a few extra screws loose in my experience," Cliff said.

The thought had occurred to Austin. With extra hands on the case, maybe they'd get to the bottom of it and he could walk away. His heart clenched at the thought.

Leaving her a second time might just kill him.

MARIA WOKE AND STRETCHED. She wasn't sure how long she'd been asleep but her head felt a little less like someone had slammed it in the door ten times. At least she had progress in one area, she thought with a frustrated sigh. She looked up at Austin, who was sitting in the same spot where she'd last seen him.

"Are you hungry?" he asked.

"I could eat," she said, thinking for the first time that she actually felt pretty hungry. Not being focused on her pain was a good thing and she considered it a good sign.

He got up and moved to the fridge where he pulled out a container of Chinese noodles.

After two minutes in the microwave he poured them onto a plate.

"Your security detail is outside," he said.

"Oh, yeah? Who'd they send?" she asked, settling into the chair next to him and then taking a bite.

"Cliff Ford," he supplied.

"Oh, good. He's really good at his job," she said after finishing chewing. "I'm glad Vic sent him. Where is he?"

"He's walking the perimeter. I have his cell if you need to talk to him," he said.

"Did he say how much trouble I'm in?" she asked with a small smile.

"He said it'll blow over." Austin dug his fork into the noodles piled on his plate.

"I was thinking that I could maybe pick his brain about my caseload, but that's probably not a good idea," she said. "I'm pretty sure he's been briefed by Vic."

Austin nodded and she was glad the earlier tension seemed to have eased. Or maybe the nap gave her a better perspective.

"That's a safe bet," he stated.

"We still don't have much to go on and all I ever do is draw blanks when I try to remember," she said. "I'm getting frustrated."

"It's okay." There was no conviction in his tone. "The more you try, the harder it'll be on you and it's only been six days."

Maria focused on finishing the rest of her food. The doctor had said the same thing but not being in control was an awful feeling. That's all a person really had was their memories, right?

"Whatever I did to you…I'm sorry," she said when she set her fork down.

"Like I said, it's nothing." He picked up their plates and tossed the few leftover bits into the trash. Then, he closed the lid.

"It doesn't seem like it," she said under her breath. And then added, "I miss Denali. I hope he's improving."

She surprised herself when a sob released and a few tears spilled down her cheeks.

"I'm sorry," she said quickly. "I don't know where that came from."

He looked up at her, so she turned to face the wall while sniffing back tears.

She sipped the coffee he'd made for her, prepared just the way she liked it.

"Can we go for a walk? My legs are sore from so much inactivity," she said.

"I'll text Cliff." He fished his cell out of his pocket before finishing his own cup and placing it inside the sink.

"Was it work? Before?" She eyed him curiously. "The reason we don't talk about anything? Was I always at work?"

"Why don't you ask Mitch DeCarlo?" He looked sorry for saying it the minute the words left his mouth. "Look. I don't mean to be… It's just. Complicated."

"So I gathered," she said under her breath as she

stood. She moved to the door and slipped into her running shoes. Movement still hurt but it felt good to be going outside.

Her hand was on the door handle, ready to go, when Austin placed his hand on the door, stopping her from opening it. His gaze was intense on her. He looked tormented and…hungry. A thousand tiny butterflies released in her stomach. Before she knew what had hit her, her back was against the door and Austin had dipped his head down and pressed his lips to hers. He tasted like the coffee he'd had a minute ago, her favorite drink. Her body ached to be touched by her husband. Memories of how intense their love-making had been assaulted her. Her hands splayed out on his chest and she could feel his rapid breathing through her fingertips. Her fingers stretched and flexed along the smooth lines of his muscled chest.

He pulled back way too fast. "That was a mistake."

"Really, Austin? Was it? You kissed your wife. I don't think anyone's going to arrest you for doing what every married couple across the nation does," she said through raspy breaths.

"When I told you that we'd been having problems before, I was serious. I don't want to take advantage of the fact that you can't remember and the doctor says that I can't bring you up-to-date. It would be so much easier if I could," he said. "But you'd feel different about me, about *this*." He kissed her again, both of his hands coming up to cup her cheeks, and her knees almost buckled.

How could that be a bad thing? She knew how her body reacted to him. She wanted him in every way possible. Maria surrendered to the moment, parting her lips so his tongue could slip inside and taste her. He'd always said that he loved the way she tasted.

He repositioned and opened his eyes. Those intense green eyes looking into her, searching…

"Did that help?" he asked, and there was so much hope in his voice that she hated to let him down. "Feel familiar? Bring anything back?"

"No. The only thing it tells me is that we have incredible chemistry," she said honestly.

"We did for a while," he muttered.

Frustration nailed her. Not knowing anything, having no connection to her life had to be much worse than any avalanche could be. Hell, she'd take anything at this point because all she knew was that every cell inside her body wanted this man but there was so much hurt in his eyes. There was no question that they still had sexual chemistry. All couldn't be lost if they still had that, could it? How bad could it be? Maybe she'd worked too much. Or they'd fought and needed to clear the air but didn't so they drifted apart. Whatever it was, they could fix it. Her body would never want a man this badly who was bad for her in any way.

"Tell me one thing. One thing can't possibly cause a flood. Give me one bit of reality to hold on to, to build on," she said, and she was practically begging. Otherwise, the frustration might just kill her.

He stood there for a long moment before he made a move to speak. "You should know that you sent me divorce papers."

He dropped his hands from her face.

"Why on earth would I do that?" she balked. "Is there someone else?"

"Yes," he said.

"What's her name?" she asked, steeling her resolve so that she could take whatever came next.

"Mitch DeCarlo."

Austin turned, opened the door and walked out.

A sharp pain pierced her chest at the look on his face. So it was her fault? She'd been the one to have an affair with someone at work? Maria searched her mind, trying to figure out how that was even possible. It was so clear to her that she was in love with Austin. That she wanted to return to the ranch and be with her husband more than she wanted to breathe.

And yet if that was true, how could there be another man involved?

At least the hurt in Austin's eyes made more sense with this new information. Maria churned the news over in her mind. Wouldn't there be some connection? Wouldn't hearing that name stir something inside her?

She stood there for a few minutes saying *Mitch DeCarlo* over and over again, wishing it would ring a bell. Earlier, she'd had a small blip when it came to him but that was nothing compared to the emotions she felt when Austin was near. She thought about the fact that Mitch's name had been familiar when she'd read it on her phone. She must not have known him for very long if she didn't have a long-term memory of him. Right?

The handsome cowboy's reaction made so much more sense to her now. She didn't want to believe she was the kind of person who could have an affair, not when she still had so many feelings for her husband. Mitch DeCarlo must not be too important to her if she didn't remember anything about him. Or could he be?

Maria had had the feeling all along that the tension between her and Austin was her fault. Now she had proof.

Maybe a walk would clear her head. As it was, her brain felt cramped. She opened the door and walked outside.

"Cliff, how are you?" Maria walked to her co-worker and shook his outstretched hand, ignoring the pain stabbing her chest at seeing Austin.

"I'm good. No hits to the head lately. Although, if I duck out on one more Little League game in the name of work Loraine is threatening to knock me upside mine," he said with a wink.

At least she remembered him. Maybe talking to him would give her a much-needed break from the tension between her and Austin. As long as she was wishing, maybe it would stir a work memory. He asked, "What about you? How are you really doing?"

"The doctor says I'm on track," she said. "I don't feel it so much. Thought a walk might clear my head."

"Fresh air might do some good," Cliff agreed.

Maria nodded and managed a smile.

"Where are we heading?" Cliff asked as Austin approached them.

She acknowledged him with a nod and he seemed content to walk behind them a couple of paces. She figured that he needed the privacy. Being around her 24/7 after she'd served him divorce papers couldn't exactly be pleasant. For the life of her, she couldn't imagine why she'd want to break up. And he wasn't talking. He'd said it was for her health.

"Let's take Veterans Drive," she said, thinking they could come in at a different angle from where they found the dog last time. There'd be people everywhere this time of day, so it would be easy to blend in with the crowd.

"Near Zilker Park. Nice. It's beautiful this time of year," he said.

They were talking about everything but work, which was fine. She'd vowed that she wouldn't be the one to bring it up first even though a thousand questions racked her brain.

"How's Loraine?" she asked, remembering his wife's name.

"She's good. You know how it is with the little ones running around…" He issued an awkward pause. "Sorry about that. I forgot about…"

"What?"

"Nothing," he quickly said, eyes forward, focused on the patch of ground two feet in front of them.

"If one more person tells me that it's nothing I might actually scream," she stated.

He apologized again.

"You don't have to be sorry," she said.

"It must be hell. Not being able to remember," he acknowledged.

"Believe me, it is."

It was starting to get dark and there was a crisp edge to the air. Downtown was alive with people, college students, professionals. There was so much foot traffic it was like an ant farm and was starting to feel crowded. But then a crowd was a good thing at a time like this, she thought. Was this her life? How could it be? Everything felt so foreign, so alone and so different from what she really wanted.

Being on the trail should comfort her. Wasn't that her routine? She'd always been an early riser, a runner. Wasn't that the reason she kept her shoes by the door?

"Well, how are the kids?" she asked.

"Mikey's good. He's getting big, playing soccer and baseball. Janie is sweet as ever and the baby… she's sweet but this no-sleep business is getting to me," he said with an exaggerated expression.

The baby? She thought he had two kids. Maria

didn't say anything at first. The third must've slipped her mind. *Great.*

"How old is she now?" she finally asked.

"Four months," he said with the pride only a loving father could possess.

"Wow, I didn't realize so much time had gone by," she said.

"Loraine's a trouper. She's the one home all day, staying up most of the night," he said. "I do what I can to help her but she's like Superwoman when it comes to the kids."

"Have you been working a lot of OT lately?" she asked, trying to sound casual but wondering who was picking up her slack.

"Not too bad," was all he said.

She was still trying to get over the fact that his wife had had another baby. And that pretty much meant that the last year of her life was completely gone. Her thoughts wound back to Mitch DeCarlo. Was he the reason that she was getting a divorce from Austin? Had it gotten so bad between them that all the love she felt right now was gone? She could hardly imagine it but the evidence was hard to dispute.

The trio had wandered onto the Lady Bird not far from Zilker Park and the crowd didn't thin. It seemed like there was always a lot of foot traffic in Austin—it was always pedestrian rush hour, save for the super early hours of the morning when there were only a few joggers sprinkled around the city.

Cliff didn't seem to be too shocked that her husband was around. Wouldn't someone from work know her well enough to realize that she was separated and, if she could believe the handsome rancher, about to be divorced?

She looked over at Cliff, who was wearing a puzzled expression.

"What is it? What's wrong?" she asked.

"I think that's the most we've said to each other in more than a year," he said.

"Seriously?"

"Yeah, I mean, you're not much of a talker. Not after…" He made that same gesture with his hands. "You know, life got *real* for you."

"Sorry about that," she said, figuring she'd damaged that relationship, too. She was really racking them up.

"No. It's no trouble. I mean, we all knew you were going through a lot, so we gave you space," he said.

"Yeah, separations are hard," she said, figuring he was talking about her marriage.

"That, too," he said, sounding surprised that she hadn't caught on. From their conversation so far, she gathered that she'd been through something traumatic. The rancher, her husband, seemed like he wanted to tell her something to stir her memories, but he was afraid to cause more trauma. If she could figure out what happened a year ago, she could possibly unlock her memories.

A snap, like popping open a Coke can, came from

the right followed by a long fizzing sound and so much smoke that Maria couldn't see her hand in front of her face. Her eyes watered and burned as she tried to push her way out of the heavy fog, desperate to break through and find clean air. She coughed and wheezed, her throat feeling like someone had lit a blaze inside.

She coughed again and it felt like her throat was closing up on her. She dropped to the cement, banging her knees in the process.

White smoke was everywhere and it felt like liquid was coming out of every pore…her nose, her eyes. Everywhere but her mouth, which felt like she was chewing on sandpaper. A tacky taste had her gagging as she felt her way around, trying to find something to grab onto that could bring her out of the fog. She tucked her chin to her chest and pulled her shirt up to her eyes, trying to filter the air.

She tried to scream but ended up in a coughing fit instead, gagging on mucus lodged in the back of her throat. It felt like her tonsils were on fire.

Strong hands gripped her from the ground where she was on all fours, clawing for purchase on the cement. She was beginning to feel disoriented and nauseous. Her eyes itched and all she could think about was scratching, finding some kind of relief for the intense burn.

The next thing she knew she was being hauled up to her feet and moved out of the fog. She stumbled, trying to keep pace, but fell to the ground again.

Those same familiar hands tugged on her shirt until they took hold of her arms again.

There was a struggle going on behind her, male voices that she couldn't quite make out through ears that itched incessantly.

And then she heard the unmistakable crack of a gun.

Chapter Nine

Maria strained to get a visual on the person dragging her out of the smoke. She tried to speak but only coughed more. The next thing she knew she was on the ground alongside the male figure who'd saved her. His hands had felt so familiar and instinct said they belonged to Austin.

Either way, both of them were gasping for oxygen as the sounds of police sirens pierced the air.

Within a few seconds, voices surrounded both her and the male figure next to her in a circle. She squinted through blurry eyes well enough to see that it was Austin lying beside her and relief washed over her. They were on their backs and neither seemed able to move.

"You're going to be okay. Help is on the way," one of the voices said as the sirens drew near.

The city of Austin had a solid police presence and she was never more grateful for that fact than now.

Maria tried to sit up and get a visual on Cliff. It was no use. Her eyes were too blurry and she

YOUR PARTICIPATION IS REQUESTED!

Dear Reader,

Since you are a lover of our books – we would like to get to know you!

Inside you will find a short Reader's Survey. Sharing your answers with us will help our editorial staff understand who you are and what activities you enjoy.

To thank you for your participation, we would like to send you 2 books and 2 gifts – **ABSOLUTELY FREE!**

Enjoy your gifts with our appreciation,

Pam Powers

SEE INSIDE FOR READER'S SURVEY

For Your Reading Pleasure...

We'll send you 2 books and 2 gifts
ABSOLUTELY FREE
just for completing our Reader's Survey!

YOUR READER'S SURVEY
"THANK YOU" FREE GIFTS INCLUDE:
▶ **2 FREE books**
▶ **2 lovely surprise gifts**

PLEASE FILL IN THE CIRCLES COMPLETELY TO RESPOND

1) What type of fiction books do you enjoy reading? (Check all that apply)
- ○ Suspense/Thrillers
- ○ Action/Adventure
- ○ Modern-day Romances
- ○ Historical Romance
- ○ Humor
- ○ Paranormal Romance

2) What attracted you most to the last fiction book you purchased on impulse?
- ○ The Title
- ○ The Cover
- ○ The Author
- ○ The Story

3) What is usually the greatest influencer when you <u>plan</u> to buy a book?
- ○ Advertising
- ○ Referral
- ○ Book Review

4) How often do you access the internet?
- ○ Daily
- ○ Weekly
- ○ Monthly
- ○ Rarely or never

5) How many NEW paperback fiction novels have you purchased in the past 3 months?
- ○ 0 - 2
- ○ 3 - 6
- ○ 7 or more

YES! I have completed the Reader's Survey. Please send me 2 FREE books and 2 FREE gifts (gifts are worth about $10 retail). I understand that I am under no obligation to purchase any books, as explained on the back of this card.

❏ I prefer the regular-print edition
182/382 HDL GLY5

❏ I prefer the larger-print edition
199/399 HDL GLY5

FIRST NAME   LAST NAME

ADDRESS

APT.#   CITY

STATE/PROV.   ZIP/POSTAL CODE

HI-817-SUR17

READER SERVICE—Here's how it works:

◀ If offer card is missing write to: Reader Service, P.O. Box 1341, Buffalo, NY 14240-8531 or visit www.ReaderService.com ▶

BUSINESS REPLY MAIL
FIRST-CLASS MAIL   PERMIT NO. 717   BUFFALO, NY

POSTAGE WILL BE PAID BY ADDRESSEE

READER SERVICE
PO BOX 1341
BUFFALO NY 14240-8571

NO POSTAGE
NECESSARY
IF MAILED
IN THE
UNITED STATES

couldn't stop coughing. She'd lost the sound of his voice somewhere in the thick of the struggle.

The next thing she knew an oxygen mask was being placed over her nose and mouth. She took in a couple of deep breaths before she tried to stand.

"That's not a good idea right now." An EMT's face blocked her view. She glanced toward Austin who was already pushing to his feet.

Maria needed to see Cliff. She'd lost all contact inside the smoke bomb and she wanted to make sure he was being attended to.

"This is Lieutenant Danville of APD and I need all onlookers to clear the area," came a strong male voice over a PA system. She glanced around through burning eyes and realized a small crowd had gathered.

She pulled the mask up far enough to ask, "My partner was with us. Is he okay?"

The EMT immediately repositioned the mouth covering on her face as she coughed.

"I'm not sure, ma'am. I can ask for you if you'll keep this on," he stated.

She was already nodding and making an effort to speak again.

"Hold on. Just let me make sure you're good to go," he said. The EMT's shirt had the name Roger embroidered above the pocket.

Maria lifted the mouthpiece again and coughed. "Roger, my partner might be lying in that fog, taking his last breath. So, I'm not keeping this thing on and sitting here doing nothing until I know that he's out of there safely." Her voice was scratchy and sounded like she'd swallowed fire but she didn't care. At this point, all she cared about was making sure that Cliff had been found and that bullet, meant for her, hadn't done any damage to her friend. He had a wife and kids to go home to.

And then she saw the stretcher and an EMT straddled over a lifeless body as he hammered a man's chest—a man who could only be Cliff—counting beats as he tried to pump air into his lungs. The EMT pinched the bridge of Cliff's nose and blew measured breaths into his mouth.

Roger said something to her, something like an affirmation, but his voice was distant as a few memories from the past assaulted Maria. Guilt fisted her chest as she remembered the incident with her training officer, Carl Sullivan, during her rookie year of police work. He'd been the one driving when they'd chased a suspect to the Natural Bridge Caverns north of the city.

The perp had abandoned this old turquoise blue Chevy with a license plate so bent it had been impossible to read and ran inside the dark cave. It struck her as odd what the mind chose to remember in times like these, she thought.

The place had been closed to the public but they'd chased the perp into the caverns, believing that he was alone. Two against one were odds that Carl had always bet on. Adrenaline had had Maria's legs pumping to keep up with her athletic training officer.

Carl had ordered Maria to call for backup, which forced her to slow down as she radioed in the request. She received confirmation that someone was ten minutes away, possibly eight as she rejoined the chase. Carl had charged ahead, flashlight and weapon leading the way, just as she'd practiced dozens of times in scenarios training.

She'd followed Carl and the perp into the cavern as her heart pounded against her ribs. There was no way she planned to be the weak link. Being a woman in law enforcement already gave her an uphill battle to win her colleagues' respect. The men didn't trust each other easily and she knew going in that she'd have a more difficult time winning their respect as a woman. Maria had been up for the challenge.

Carl had been ambushed at the same time she caught up with him. The perp had slammed a rock into Carl's head, the force of the blow killing him instantly, and then used Carl's service revolver to try to shoot Maria. She'd repositioned behind a large calcium formation and the bullet had pinged past so close to her ear that she swore she could hear the whistle ringing inside her head for weeks afterward. Before she could get a good visual on the perp, she heard an unfamiliar voice behind her. She was essentially sandwiched in between two escaped convicts.

If backup hadn't arrived when it had and scared

them off, she'd be dead. Her TO Carl Sullivan had been her mentor. He and his wife had been expecting their first child. And murder had followed Maria once again.

Pain engulfed her, leaving her feeling like she was on fire from the inside out. It was all starting to come back as she breathed into the plastic mask covering her face. There was such a thin piece of material between clean air and more of that fog that made her lungs ache.

Needless to say, the perps had disappeared from the cavern. She'd discharged her weapon and had been put on desk duty pending internal investigation and psychological evaluation. In the coffee room before her shift, she'd heard another officer make a snide remark about hoping to hell that she wasn't assigned to him. She'd rounded the corner and brushed past him to make sure he knew she'd heard him. He'd apologized and she accepted. She'd never breathed another word about the incident and had shoved down her feelings of how much it had hurt. But she knew that he'd been right about her. She was unlucky to those she cared most about.

More memories crashed down around her. Memories of her life with Austin at the ranch, of the baby they'd lost. She remembered how she and Austin had drifted apart, the long walks she'd taken, the conversations that had been left on the tip of her tongue but never said.

She'd been seven months pregnant. They'd picked out a name, Raina. The nursery had been almost finished.

And then the cramps had come, the blood…the loss.

More bad luck, people had said. And she'd realized that it wasn't bad luck at all. It was *her* luck.

AUSTIN LEANED HIS head back against the headrest of the police cruiser as he went through the events. He, Maria and Cliff had been ambushed by someone using tear gas. Whoever did this had military skills. Things hadn't gone as the attacker had expected and Austin figured he was at least part of the reason. He'd been hanging back to give Maria and Cliff a chance to talk and the attacker must not have realized that he was with them. An attack in broad daylight with people everywhere meant this guy was escalating.

Cliff was already at the hospital and, thankfully, not the morgue. He was in great physical shape and that would most likely save his life.

The officer parked the vehicle and escorted them upstairs to Maria's loft. Austin figured he could handle everything from here, but the officer would have orders to stay with them and Austin had no plans to make the man's job more difficult than it already was by arguing.

"You're welcome to come inside," Austin said to

the uniformed officer who'd introduced himself as Edward Long.

"My SO asked me to check the place out," Officer Long said. "If you don't mind, I'd like to go in first."

Maria unlocked and opened the door.

"Be my guest." Austin held his hand out, palm up after stepping inside. "Let me know if there's anything you need from us."

"I'd appreciate it if you'd stay near the door until I signal," Officer Long said.

"You got it," Austin agreed. Compliance would go a long way toward gaining cooperation should they need it down the road and with the way the situation was escalating, they just might.

"I need to call Vic and give him an update," Maria said, palming her cell as soon as Officer Long gave them the all clear. There was something different about her since the latest attack and Austin wondered if memories were surfacing. She'd been quiet in the back of the cruiser on the way to the loft.

"That's a good idea," Austin agreed. "But I'm taking you to the ranch." He almost said the word *home* instead of ranch. He'd caught himself before making the mistake.

"I'm starting to remember a few things." She stepped into the kitchen and then spun around to face him. "So, let's think this through for a minute before I pitch it to my boss. There's enough security and everything's already in place." She glanced up at him. "Overall, it's a good idea. However—"

"I know there's something going on there but that's about my parents. Whoever is behind it, and believe me when I say we'll figure it out soon enough, they don't want anything to do with you," he said. "Besides, after we found Denali they have to know that we're onto them. Everyone's watching and security is even tighter. The place is on lockdown so no one unfamiliar is getting past the gate."

"I got so wrapped up in the last couple of hours I forgot to ask about Denali. Has there been any word?" she asked, and her voice was raw and husky from the smoke she'd inhaled.

"Dallas texted that he's in bad condition but stable for now. I'd like to be near him...in case—" He couldn't say the rest, the unthinkable, that anything could happen to the family dog. Denali had been Austin's near-constant companion, especially during all those late nights after Maria had left.

"It'll be easier for you to keep an eye on ranch business, too," she said. "If you're sure that you want me around."

"I've come this far," he said, not sure how to take that. Had she remembered something? Her eyes said she had. "I have plans to see this through if you'll allow me."

"I'd like that." She held up her cell. "I'll just get Vic on the phone and update him on our plans."

Vic answered on the first ring. Maria introduced him to Austin after putting the call on speaker. Then, she briefed her boss about the situation with Cliff.

Her tone was controlled and intense as she focused on relaying facts. Austin remembered how much he'd admired her dedication to her job, to her cases. He'd always understood on some level that her devotion had come out of her need to give others the justice she never had for her mother. For herself.

"You're going into protective custody," Vic said after a long pause. There was real panic in his voice and Austin could tell that he cared about Maria and his agents. As much as he wanted to point a finger at someone, anyone, for Maria's late nights at work, he'd heard Vic tell her several times to pull back.

"That could take time to set up the right place," Austin said. "I'd rather take her back to the ranch. We have the best security team available and especially given such short notice. I think it's the safest place for her under the circumstances and it'll be easier to control the environment around her."

This wasn't the time to bring up the fact that there was a murderer who had access to the ranch. He and his brothers had begun to suspect Uncle Ezra, but he'd been with Aunt Bea the night of their parents' murders. She'd given him an alibi and thanks to the tension that had always been between the two, her word could be trusted. She wouldn't take something like that lightly no matter how much she disliked her brother. And the two had been at odds since long before Austin could remember.

The silence on the other end of the phone hopefully meant that Vic was considering supporting the idea.

"I'll send someone as extra help," Vic said on a sharp sigh.

"That's not necessary," Maria said. She'd started shaking her head the minute her boss started speaking.

Austin held his hand up and caught her gaze. "I'm fine with it. We can always use more eyes on the situation. Just send me a name and I'll have him cleared with my security team."

"Will do," Vic said. "I'll see who I have and send them over. I'll arrange for Officer Long to escort you to your premises."

"The address will be on your phone as soon as we hang up," Austin said. Cooperating with Vic would help her career in the long run. "Any chance I can run her into the office tomorrow to take a look at her caseload? There might be a direct link between these attacks and her cases."

A heavy sigh came through the line.

"I'll need her statement anyway. I'll work something out with Internal Affairs so she can come in," Vic said. "Take care of her in the meantime."

"I can take care of myself," Maria said, her back stiffening as her stubborn streak kicked into gear.

Austin couldn't help but crack a smile.

"When you're running at a hundred percent I have no doubt that's true. Right now, you're injured and I'm not visiting another agent in the hospital if I have anything to say about it," Vic said slowly and with authority. "And let me remind you that I'm still your boss."

He was right and Maria seemed to know that when she bit her lip instead of putting up more of an argument.

Austin was glad she didn't try to push their luck. They'd scored a major victory in getting her boss to agree to the ranch. "We'll be in constant contact as we work together to figure this out."

"Good." Vic seemed to be relaxing a little. Not much. But a little. "Take care of yourself, Maria. You're one of, if not *the* best agent I have and I don't want anything else happening to you."

The compliment seemed to catch her off guard. "You got it, chief. No more bad guys catching up to me."

She ended the call and set her phone on the counter. "I'll just pack a few things and we can head out."

Her phone buzzed a minute later, indicating that she had a text.

"Vic is putting Officer Long on the first watch, so he'll be the one to meet with your security," she said, and then she pulled out a duffel bag.

Austin nodded and took in a sharp breath.

They were going home.

THIS PLACE IS exactly the same as I remember it," Maria said somberly as Austin pulled into the garage and parked. There was a flicker of something that looked a lot like hope in her eyes but it disappeared like a star blinking in the night.

"It hasn't been *that* long since you were here," he said. Something had changed in her and Austin was still trying to pinpoint it as the cruiser parked in front of the house.

He closed the garage door and led her into the kitchen. Officer Long was already at the front door, so Austin showed him in.

"Can I get you a cup of coffee?" Austin asked the officer.

"Yes, sir," Officer Long said. "Mind if I take a look around?"

"Be my guest. I'll put on a fresh pot." Austin went to the kitchen as the officer moved to the sliding glass door to the patio.

"I remember where the guest bedroom is. I'll just put my things in there." Maria motioned toward the hallway opposite the master.

"Just set your bag down there," he said, pointing next to the couch in the living room. She'd have to walk past the nursery to get to the guest room and he didn't want that to hit her out of the blue, especially since she didn't seem to remember.

She paused for a second like she was about to argue but then did as he'd asked.

"You want a cup of coffee?" he asked.

"Absolutely," she said.

"Let me get Officer Long set up here," Austin said, pulling the carafe from the base.

"I'll take that in a to-go cup if you have one," Officer Long said. "There's more security here than I've ever seen and you probably don't need me but I'd like to take a look around the property anyway."

"I'll get Gideon Fisher, our head of security, to fix you right up with whatever you need," Austin said before firing off a text. He poured three cups of coffee, one in a to-go mug as requested, and passed them out.

Long had barely taken his first sip when Gideon knocked on the door. Austin let him in and introduced him to the officer.

Within a minute the pair was gone, leaving an awkward silence in their wake.

"You're welcome to sleep in our…in *the* master bedroom," Austin corrected.

"I can't kick you out of your bed." Maria gripped her mug like it was precious metal.

"It's fine. Half the time I fall asleep in my office or on the couch," he said.

"Everything okay with you?" she asked, really looking at him.

"You already know that I have a lot going on with the calves." He shrugged off her question.

"Since when did you stop sleeping?" she asked.

"The ranch has been busy since Mom and Dad died," he said.

"I'm so sorry about your parents. I know how close you and your family are. What really happened?"

"I already told you," he said, defensively.

"Since then," she clarified. "Maybe I can take a look at Tommy's notes? Offer a fresh perspective."

"Don't worry about it. You have enough on your plate," he said. And then he looked at her. She seemed eager to talk about something besides her own problems for a change. If him opening up a little could break some of the tension between them, he'd give it a shot.

"At this point, I'd welcome the distraction," she said. "My brain is still trying to process what happened and it's hard to think while I'm so worried about Cliff."

"I'll tell you as much as I know but I can see if Tommy will let you take a look at the file. I'm sure he'd appreciate another perspective," Austin said. It felt good to be home again after being gone for a week.

"How about Joshua? Think I can speak to him? I mean, would he want to talk to me?" she asked, clearly walking on eggshells.

"You're part of the family here, Maria. A piece of paper won't change that," he said, and there was so much going on inside her head he could almost hear the kinetic energy pinging.

She took a sip of coffee and didn't immediately look at him. "After this latest attempt on my life, a few things came back to me."

"Like what?" He stared at his coffee mug.

"We lost a baby, and that's why you don't want me to stay in the guest room. I'd have to walk past her…" He could feel her eyes on him but he didn't give away his response. "That's when things between us fell apart, isn't it?"

He nodded but kept his gaze focused on the handle of his coffee mug.

"I'm sorry," she said. "It was my fault. I must've exercised too much or had too much stress. I should've stopped working…"

"There you go again," he said, not bothering to mask his frustration. "How strong could we have been if we couldn't get through our first real problem together? You were right to walk away."

He glanced up in time to see the hurt in her eyes. Hurt that he put there. He wanted to apologize but stopped short when her hand came up.

"I'm going to lie down. My offer still stands if you want my help with your parents' case. They were good people and didn't deserve what happened to them," she said, and her voice had that cold, all-business edge to it.

"Maria—"

"Don't, Austin. An apology isn't necessary at this point." She turned and walked away, picking up her bag before heading down the hallway to the guest room. She didn't so much as flinch as she walked past what would have been their daughter's room.

Chapter Ten

By morning, Maria was all business. She wore dark jeans and a navy blue V-neck short-sleeved shirt. Her hair was tied back neatly in a ponytail.

"I made coffee," Austin said through a yawn. He'd never really been a morning person and his brothers had had a field day with that considering they'd been born on a ranch. It didn't help that he'd spent most of the night alternating between thoughts of her case and the few kisses they'd shared—kisses that had heated his blood faster than a boiling pot. The latter were inappropriate thoughts under the circumstances and yet this was Maria, his wife, and he could admit to having an overload of nostalgia when she was near. Having her home felt right on many levels but he re-minded himself not to confuse circumstance with her making a decision to return.

Maria didn't comment as she walked over to the counter. Tension radiated off of her in waves and it had nothing to do with her case. That familiar vibe was her making sure he knew personal chatter was off the table.

"I'm sorry about last night. I was a jerk," Austin said, handing her a mug, her mug.

"It's no problem at all," she said so casually that he almost missed the note of pain in her voice.

"Do you mind?" he asked, taking the pot from her.

She stood there, staring at the cabinet, while he filled their two mugs.

"When you closed up on me before, I didn't know what to do so I left you alone," he said, searching for the right words. "I don't think I ever apologized for my actions."

"What actions?" she shot back.

The words had the effect of a bullet chipping away a piece of his bone. The truth had a way of cutting to the core.

"I deserve that," he admitted. "It seems like your memories have come back and I have divorce papers on my desk that you've been waiting for me to sign."

She started to say something but he stopped her.

"I intend to sign them, don't worry. I just can't let you walk away without knowing that I never intended to hurt you," he said, and he touched her arm.

She stiffened but then blew out a breath and looked as though it took great effort to force herself to relax her tight shoulders.

"It was as much my fault as it was yours," she said. "I could've been the one to apologize just as easily as you or start the conversation we needed to

have. Don't blame yourself. Now, if you don't mind.
I'd really like that cup of coffee. We have a lot of
work to do today. Unless you need to hang back
here at the ranch."

"Did you remember anything about your cases?"
he asked.

"No, and I only have pieces of my personal life.
Suffice it to say, I know enough to stop asking questions about what happened between the two of us,"
she said stiffly. "And, like I already said, you can
bail anytime you want."

"I already said that I plan to see this thing
through." The chill she put in the air was a defense
mechanism. He could see that now. Maybe if he'd
figured it out before, things wouldn't have fallen
apart between them. Reliving the past wouldn't
change a thing about their current circumstances.

"Are you sure? I can always tag a ride with…who
did Vic send over last night?" she asked.

"Mitch DeCarlo."

Her hand visibly shook as she tried to hide the
effect the news was having on her. Austin knew her
well enough to know that would be a blow.

"Mitch is here?" she asked.

"He's outside walking the perimeter." It had taken
every bit of Austin's self-control *not* to say something
to Mitch when he'd knocked on the door last night.
But the man had apologized fifty times and Austin
had decided to put his own feelings about the con-

flict of interest and the fact that he was dating his wife on the back burner.

"I need to speak to him," she said.

"I'll bet you do," was all Austin said before walking out of the room.

RELIEF WASHED OVER Maria and her shoulders sagged when Austin shut the door to the master bedroom. It had taken all the energy she could muster to put on her game face this morning and shove down the emotions threatening to drop her to her knees.

Being in the house again brought a flood of memories of her pregnancy. Even though Raina had never taken a breath outside the womb Maria felt like she'd become a mother the first time that little girl kicked inside her.

She caught herself touching her stomach at the memory. There was no use. Raina was gone. Emotions threatened to overwhelm her like pelting rain from a heavy thunderstorm. All Maria's insecurities crashed down around her as the dark cloud hovering over her returned, curling its outstretched fingers around her, suffocating her. How naive had she been to think that she and Austin could have a real life together, that all the tragedy was behind her and not stalking her like prey?

And she was literally being stalked now. Clouds were thickening and the walls felt like they were closing in.

There wasn't much she could do about her relationship with Austin. She'd hurt him in the worst possible way. The gentleman in him wouldn't let him quit until this whole case was behind her. Maybe that was the closure he needed in order to move on. In the meantime, there was a predator loose and she had every intention of making sure he was locked away forever. And then she'd finally let Austin O'Brien go so he could move on with his life. Her heart ached again at the thought of walking away from him but she had enough love for him to know that he didn't deserve the kind of misery that would surely follow her for the rest of her life. Maria was better at helping other families find justice and that wasn't a bad role to play.

Pain seared her heart. Would she ever stop loving Austin? The sad truth was that she couldn't imagine loving a man more than him. They'd been happy once. Crazy in love. And that memory would have to carry her for the rest of her life.

She looked down and realized that her hand had been on her stomach the whole time she thought about him.

A shadow moved behind the front door. She knew exactly what she had to do.

"Mitch," Maria said, walking outside with a grip on her coffee mug so tight she feared she might crack the handle. Let the mug shatter, she thought. Then, it would be more in line with her heart.

Mitch made a move toward her and she stopped him from hugging her on the porch of the home she'd shared with her husband. The man she was still married to.

"We need to talk," she said.

"It's been killing me to walk away and not contact you," Mitch said. "I wanted to be there for you, but I know how you feel about anyone at work knowing what's going on between us."

Maria really was confused. Hearing Mitch's name had caused the nagging feeling she'd had in the back of her mind to surface. He was the "thing" she'd been forgetting. But not because she loved him. She remembered that she'd planned on having a conversation with him about her still being in love with her husband. Standing there, seeing the look of hope in Mitch's eyes, made her keenly aware of the fact that she was about to hurt someone else.

Surely he'd understand. Until Maria pulled her life together, she didn't need to be involved with anyone.

"Based on your reaction, I'm guessing you don't remember what we meant to each other," he said, and he sounded wounded.

Damn.

"That's what we need to discuss," she said, taking in a fortifying breath.

"Does that mean you're ready to go public with our relationship?" he asked, and there was an eager quality to his tone that made her feel like she was about to shatter his feelings. "Because I think that's a great idea. I mean, the timing could be a little better for me work-wise since I'm up for the promotion—"

"Which I think *you* should take," she said.

Mitch stood there, staring at her for a long moment. He had a stocky build, tight-cut sandy-blond hair and too-serious expression. There was no comparison between Mitch and Austin and the fact that Mitch was opposite was most likely the initial attraction and not that they had anything in common besides being dedicated to the job.

"I thought we agreed this move would be good for both of us." He eyed her up and down as he seemed to connect the dots to what she'd implied.

Maria shook her head. "I never said that."

"But I distinctly remember you saying that a move like this would be good for our future," he said.

"I said it would be good for *your* future. And I still believe that," she clarified. When he'd first lumped her into the category of "being on board" with his choice as though it had belonged to the two of them she hadn't corrected him. He'd been excited and she figured their short-lived fling would be left in the dust as soon as he made it through the interview process. Half the reason she'd finally accepted his request for a date was because she'd believed that it might help give her closure from Austin. A year had passed and Maria had still been trying to cover the hole left in her chest when she'd parted ways with her husband. Nothing in her world had felt right since that day and going out with Mitch had been a way to test the waters to see if she was ready to date.

It hadn't taken long to realize that she wasn't. Dating a coworker had been an idiotic move because she had to be more delicate about untangling herself. Mitch hadn't read the signs, either.

"You still haven't answered my question," Mitch said, and she didn't have to be an investigator to pick up on the agitation in his voice.

"Remind me what you asked," she said, snapping back to the present. If she kept looking backward she'd eventually run into a wall. That statement pretty much covered everything in the last year.

"Did you ever have feelings for me?" Mitch asked, and then turned his back to her. "Never mind. I sound like a needy kid when I ask that."

Maria didn't know what to say, so she kept quiet. Mitch was good at talking. And she was the opposite.

"I just thought *we* had a plan." He spun around to face her. She'd expected to see hurt in his eyes but it was more like disappointment, like he wanted coffee but all someone had was tea.

"I'm sorry," she said to him, thinking that she needed to say those words to Austin instead. She couldn't imagine him hearing that she was dating from someone else and many of his actions were starting to make more sense to her now. "We've barely been dating."

"How long does it take for you to know that you want be with someone?" he shot back, a little more fire in his eyes this time.

"I don't know. More than a couple dates," she said,

holding her ground. She didn't want to give him the impression that he could change her mind.

"Sure, we'd only gone out on a couple of dates but we've known each other much longer. It's not like we only just met," he stated.

"True." She couldn't deny that part, but they'd never spent time together in real life—life outside of the job. Maybe there'd been some comfort in dating someone who understood her work schedule. Or at least that's what she'd believed. Relationships at work were taboo and she assumed that she'd be safe. And then Mitch had thrown her the curveball of making plans for a future together.

Not a shock to anyone who knew her, talking about emotions wasn't really her thing. She'd believed there'd be some safety in spending time with a man like Mitch given that he wasn't her usual type. Unfortunately, the same couldn't be said for him and he didn't seem to mind spending time with a woman who rarely spoke. "I apologize if I misled you. It's just that I didn't think we were taking a couple of dates seriously."

His face turned beet red.

"I guess *we* weren't," he said sarcastically.

She needed to keep her cool. He was obviously hurting, or maybe just felt scorned. Either way, it was her fault. She should've put a stop to his advances after the first date. That's all it had taken for her to realize her mistake.

"Does Vic know?" she asked, worried that her career could be over if word got out.

"No, I only told one friend," he said and then came, "Is that what you're concerned about?" There was real anger in his tone now. "Work?"

"I guess I thought this wouldn't be good for either one of our careers—"

"No, Vic doesn't know. Do you really think he'd send me out here if he did?" Mitch practically shouted.

"No, I—"

"Furthermore, I wouldn't care if he did. I actually thought we had something special," he said as she walked away from the house. The last thing she needed was for Austin to get involved and he would if he heard the screaming or believed that she wasn't being treated well. Cowboy Code or something, but it had been good at seducing her.

"I already said that I'm sorry, Mitch," she said, making sure he followed.

"A job is easier to find than someone you want to spend the rest of your life with," Mitch said.

"What?" Maria balked.

"Fine. There. I said it. I was planning to ask you to marry me," he said.

And now it was her turn to have a red face. And she felt really bad for not paying more attention to his feelings.

"Mitch—"

His hand came up. "Don't say it. It's clear to me

that you're still in love with your ex." He glanced around. "I'll ask for a new assignment."

Maria took in a breath, unsure what to say next. Was she still in love with Austin? Yes. Had she gotten over him? That was easy—no.

"But let me ask one thing before I go," he said, and she wasn't real sure she wanted to hear what he was about to say. "Why'd you move out? Why'd you leave him when it's so obvious to me now that you're still in love with him?"

"Mitch—"

"I feel like an idiot, so don't make it worse by showing me how little you care about me," he said.

"That's not true. I do care," she said and meant it. Love? Marriage? Her feelings had only run that deep for one man—and look how that turned out.

Mitch stormed off mumbling something about walking the perimeter while making a call to Vic. There'd been so much hurt in Mitch's eyes, hurt that she put there, proving once again that being involved with her was toxic to the other person. In Mitch's case, it seemed more like embarrassed hurt than being truly wounded, but it was her fault no matter how she categorized it.

The front door swung open with a clank and Austin stepped outside, his expression saying that he was unaware of the heavy conversation that had taken place only a few seconds ago.

"If you want to head to the office today, we should

go," he said, and his voice was distant. Not so much his tone but the emotions in it.

"Let me grab my purse," she said before retrieving the bag and then following him to his truck, still shocked by Mitch's revelation.

Was she really that unaware of other people's feelings?

In short? Yes. And Austin would be so much better off without her. Based on his tight expression he seemed to realize it, too.

MARIA SWIPED HER BADGE. A red light blinked back at her. She tried again with the same result. *Great.* Her badge had been temporarily deactivated, so she had to be buzzed into the regional field office at 111 Justice Street.

Walking inside the lobby area, Maria finally felt in her element.

Personal memories were coming back in pieces and she didn't exactly like what she saw so far. To make matters worse, Austin had been quiet on the ride over and she wondered if he'd overheard any of her fight with Mitch. Surely not, but then a year was a long time. Maybe he'd changed. Or maybe she didn't know him as well as she once thought.

"Good to see you, Maria," Janet Alderman at the reception desk said with a smile. Janet was petite, thin and dressed like she was starring in a *Men in Black* movie. It was meant to be funny and Maria usually saw the humor. Janet also enjoyed the dark suits and black sunglasses sitting on top of her head that were tucked into her French braid.

"I can't wait to get back to work," Maria admitted before introducing Janet to Austin.

Her new coworker blushed as she popped to her feet and twirled the end of her braid around her finger. Was she flirting? Leave it to Janet to rile up Maria's jealousy—jealousy she had no right to own. Mitch's accusation wound through her thoughts, the one about her still being in love with her ex. Not that it mattered because she most certainly wasn't in love with Mitch.

"It's not the same around here without you," Janet said, looping their arms before lowering her voice. "And why have I never met this guy before?"

Now it was Maria's turn to blush. "Haven't had a chance to bring him around, I guess."

It was partially true.

Relief washed over Maria as she walked the familiar halls toward her work area. It felt good to be back at work and to have something to focus on besides her personal life, which felt like it had crumbled around her.

"Glad you could stop by to give your statement." Vic's voice boomed from his office as soon as they rounded the corner. He spoke louder than usual and she saw why a second later. A man in a suit stood at his doorway and she assumed the guy was from Internal Affairs.

"You want to wait out here?" she asked Austin.

Her desk was tidy. Everything was kept on computers now anyway. And she couldn't wait to dig through her electronic files. But first, she'd need to cover a base with her boss.

"Coffee?" she asked Austin.

He nodded.

"Break room is right back there." She motioned toward the opposite wall to Vic's office.

"I don't mind showing him," Janet chirped. Normally, Maria liked her coworker's perkiness. Why was it suddenly so irritating?

"Fine. This shouldn't take more than ten minutes," Maria said to Janet and she wasn't sure why she'd clarified a time frame. She chalked it up to old feelings, put on a smile and walked toward Vic's office.

"No problem. Take your time," Janet said. "I'll take care of your friend."

Maria shot Austin a look of apology at the overt flirting, but he seemed too focused on his own thoughts to really notice.

The man in the suit stuck his hand out, forgoing a smile and said, "Norm Falderal."

"Maria O'Brien." She took the offering and shook.

As soon as she took a seat in Vic's office, Norm from Internal Affairs closed the door.

Chapter Eleven

"How'd it go?" Austin asked, handing Maria a cup of coffee as she plopped down in her chair at her desk. "That bad?"

"No. It's fine. Thank you." She took the mug. The coffee burned her throat and she liked the sensation. "It was okay. He asked pretty basic questions and I told him everything that I knew, which wasn't a lot. It's his job to try to rattle me or make me trip up, but I'm not lying about anything so it was mostly exhausting." She pinched the bridge of her nose to stave off a raging headache. Caffeine. She needed more and then she really would be okay.

Maria kept to herself the stressful part where she was asked to clarify her relationship with Mitch. Dating a coworker was against policy and she'd classified her relationship with him as camaraderie. Based on their earlier conversation, he would put it in a whole different category and she felt bad for leading him on if that's what she'd done.

Honestly, they'd only been on a handful of dates

and only after she'd filed for divorce from Austin a month ago. Mitch had misconstrued that as a real relationship. Again, she felt bad about that because she probably should've clued him in sooner and been more honest. The whole "getting serious" this soon had caught her completely off guard and she was still shell-shocked from their conversation. Thinking about it threatened to intensify her nasty headache. She took another sip of fresh brew and moved on.

"Sounds like a step in the right direction toward figuring out who's behind the attacks," he said. "Did you remember anything else while you were in there? Anything new?"

"I wish. I'm starting to get patchy stuff in my personal life but not a lot about work is coming back and I'm hoping that'll change as I go through my files," she said, straightening and setting her cup down. The headache didn't seem to want to loosen its grip and they didn't have time to waste. She pushed the on button on her desktop and the screen came to life a moment later. "I've been granted temporary access, which basically means we have about half an hour. I've also been given strict orders not to pursue any leads, not that I needed to be reminded. I have no plans to run off half-cocked after a man who seems intent on hurting me while I can't remember why."

Misjudging her relationship with Mitch wasn't exactly breeding confidence in her ability to read people or situations.

"I'm sure it's just procedure for them to remind

you. They're ticking a box to protect themselves against a potential lawsuit." He didn't say, "Should things go sour." And yet, those words hung in the air, reminding her just how much danger she was in. She was a target.

"You're right. I know that. It's just hard to feel like I'm on the outside looking in when I'm used to sitting on this side of the desk," she said.

"It's understandable," Austin stated. There was something about his words, his presence that kept her nerves below panic levels. But then, he'd always had that effect on her. There were other thoughts, less appropriate to the situation, that crept in as well and they involved his arms around her and them both in a tangle of sheets where her heart felt like she belonged.

That was a whole other slippery slope.

An hour later, she was reminded just how big her caseload was and the thought of coming back to her cases both excited her and overwhelmed her at the same time. She remembered all the late nights and long weekends and just how easy it was to slip into the role of working too much in order to set aside her personal issues. Had she been setting them aside or hiding in her work? It felt so much easier to solve other people's problems, to be able to give closure to families so they could begin healing, to make sure a person who took advantage of a child was locked away for good rather than to deal with her own emotions. Her internal battles were far more complex and harder to dissect, let alone begin to face.

By the time Vic shouted that she needed to wrap it up she'd tagged five cases. Each one had left her with the feeling that they could be potential powder kegs.

"These are the ones you want looked at closer?" Austin asked, pointing to the checkmarks.

"Yes, but that's going to be someone else's job now." She'd flagged them for her boss on the LAN and had been told that Special Agent Wheeler had been assigned to her case with Vic closely overseeing the agent's work.

"Can you open the first one?" Austin asked.

She did, ignoring the questions surfacing.

"Click through it slowly," he said, and she barely registered that he'd taken his phone out of his pocket.

"I can't—"

"*You're* not," he said.

It didn't take long for her to think about it. "This might not be a good idea, as much as I want to know—"

"Not even if it means finding the guy?" he asked in a low voice, and it sent an inappropriate shiver down her back.

Maria focused on the screen.

"You might remember something if you look at these files more in depth or if we visit a few places," he said. "I'm not saying talk to anyone or do anything stupid. It can't hurt to retrace some of your steps. Maybe something will stir and we can crack this case wide-open."

She seriously considered what he was saying. He made good points. She might be able to help the investigation. She knew Special Agent Wheeler fairly well and he would probably welcome the help if she remembered something crucial. She wouldn't have to admit to copying the files.

"Another set of eyes can't hurt," she conceded.

They spent another ten minutes clicking frames as her heart raced.

When they were done, she was eager to get back to the ranch and scrutinize the data. The more she thought about it, Austin was right. It would drive her crazy not to have the information available. It had already been bothering her that she couldn't remember anything about work. If this could help, then she would be grateful.

Before they left, she stopped in to say goodbye to Vic.

"Any idea when the doctor's planning to clear you for work again?" he asked.

"Soon, I hope." It was true. She desperately wanted to get back into her routine. "I have an appointment tomorrow."

"Keep me posted," he said.

"You know I will." Maria glanced at the candy bar on his desk. Three pieces were already gone. "Eat slowly."

"I'm in no hurry," he said. "Thanks for stopping

by. I'm pulling Wheeler off all other projects so he can focus on yours and stop this jerk."

"How's Cliff?" she asked.

Vic's desk suddenly became very interesting to him. "He's in critical condition. Doc says the next twenty-four hours are crucial."

"I thought he was doing better. Out of the woods." Emotion overwhelmed her and she had to choke back a sudden burst of tears.

"He took a turn a little after three o'clock this morning," he said.

"No," she said quietly, trying but failing to block out images of his wife and children. A few rogue tears fell despite how hard she fought. Sending Wheeler out to investigate when it should be her made her even more grateful Austin had taken pictures of the critical files. Surely she'd tucked a memory away that could help unlock this case.

"Get some rest while we nab this jerk," Vic said. "I need you back and in your usual form."

She nodded.

Austin's hand on the small of her back gave her more comfort than she should allow as she walked down the hallway. This was her home now. Work was all she had, all she cared about.

And she had to uncover the one secret that could unravel them all.

"Everything okay?" Austin asked Maria. She'd been quiet for the past half hour and he could tell that she'd been holding something inside.

"I'm fine," she said. Two words that meant the exact opposite in Austin's experience.

"Are you hungry?" he asked.

"I doubt I could eat anything," she said, staring out the window.

He hated how lost she looked. Maria was the strongest woman he knew. And her strength was sexy, an annoying little voice reminded. He quickly shut it down. Austin had met the man Tommy had said she planned to marry and the meeting had the effect he'd expected. It was real. It was clear. She'd moved on.

"Are you thinking about Cliff?" he asked.

"I can't stop. He has a wife and children. A new baby," she stated.

He took one hand off the steering wheel at the stoplight for long enough to stroke hers. She glanced toward him and her gaze dropped to his cell, which sat between them. He'd been careful to obstruct the casing from her view.

"May I?" she asked, motioning toward it.

He nodded as the light changed and he gripped the steering wheel again, keeping his gaze on the stretch of road ahead. Maybe he should've bought a new cover.

"This was always my favorite picture of us," she said, and there was a lost quality to her voice. "We were so…"

"Stupid."

"I was going to say happy," she said.

To him, they meant the same thing. He'd been stupidly in love with her.

There was a long silent pause as she studied the case of his phone.

"I'm sorry about Cliff. He's a good guy. I'm hoping that he'll pull through with no more complications," he said, needing to change the subject.

"And what if he doesn't? Then I've destroyed another family," she said.

Austin let those words sit for the rest of the ride home. Back on the ranch, he parked and Maria immediately hopped out of the truck. Words were building up inside him, words he needed to say to her, and the dam was weakening. He debated going after her. A few times she'd mentioned that losing their baby and their relationship had been her fault. And now she believed the same about Cliff.

The air needed to be cleared on that point, so he bolted out of the truck. "Hold on a minute, Maria."

She whirled around and he could see tears brimming in her eyes. She'd also been a little too good at stuffing down her emotions.

"I need to get something off my chest," he said, and a look of panic crossed her features.

"Is everything okay?" Officer Vincent, their new escort, asked.

"Yes," Maria said as she walked to the tree line and stopped, staring into the woods.

"You know what happened isn't your fault, right?"

Austin stalked behind her, not ready to let her convict herself for a crime she didn't commit. "Cliff—"

She whirled around on him, fire in her eyes. "Oh, but that's where you're wrong, Austin. It is most certainly my fault."

"And just how do you figure that?" he asked. "What did you do?"

"Directly? I wanted to go for that walk when I should've stayed in my apartment. Then Cliff wouldn't be in the hospital fighting for his life and none of this would be happening," she said. There was so much pain in her beautiful brown eyes when she looked at him.

"Let me get this straight," he began, "someone is hunting you down and *you* believe that's your fault."

"If I'd done my job in the first place, then the guy wouldn't be walking around free," she shot back.

"Not solving an investigation sooner is somehow your fault?" he asked.

"It is if I'm failing and putting others in danger." And with that, she let out a sob but quickly regained her composure.

It wasn't like Maria to show her emotions and Austin had to wonder how healthy it could be to bottle them up. He should know. He'd been doing the same thing since she'd walked out.

"I'll be in earshot if you need me," Officer Vincent said. He seemed to realize things were heating up between them.

"Thank you," Austin replied.

"We're not any closer to figuring this guy out and there's another agent watching over my shoulder who could end up hurt because—" she waved her arms around as she zeroed in on Austin "—the answer to all of this is locked somewhere inside my head and I can't reach it."

"You're being too hard on yourself," he said softly, needing to calm her down. Surely getting this worked up couldn't be good for healing. "None of this is your fault."

"That is just a flat-out lie. It's the lie I tried to tell myself when my mother was killed, when my TO was murdered, when the baby died…and when I lost you. Everything, I repeat *everything* is my fault." Her words were so intense he could immediately see those thoughts were deeply ingrained in her. "I can't do this with you, Austin. I'll meet you in the house in a few minutes."

He stood there for a helpless second, debating his next move. There had to be a way to make her see the truth, that she'd been the victim of unfortunate circumstances and hadn't done anything to bring those events on herself. "Maria, don't—"

"What? Take responsibility? Then who will, Austin?" Some of the fire had fizzled and she had a look similar to a balloon deflating. "I'm tired. And I want to look at the pictures on your phone and see if anything stirs."

"That's not a good idea right now," he said. "Not when you're being this hard on yourself."

"Cliff isn't getting any better while I'm having this—" her gaze darted around as if looking for the right words "—pity party for myself."

"You're good at what you do. I've already heard your boss say you're one of his best and trying to force memories might be dangerous," he stated.

When she didn't respond, he touched her back and could feel her shaking.

She turned toward him and started to speak, to protest, but the words looked like they died on her lips. She gazed up at him and he noticed the second her eyes turned from frustration to awareness—awareness of him standing so close, awareness of how intense the chemistry was causing electricity to ping between them, awareness of the deep need they shared.

Maria broke eye contact first.

"We're going to figure this out together and stop this jerk from hurting you or anyone else," he said, catching her gaze again.

She started to look away but seemed to decide against it when she said, "Kiss me, Austin."

"You belong to someone else," he argued.

She balked. "To who? Mitch? We dated a couple of times—"

"But he's been saying the two of you were planning a wedding."

"I'm sorry he mistook a couple of dates for feelings. I only agreed to them to try to get over you. I'm not seeing him anymore," she stated.

That was pretty much all the encouragement he needed. He cupped her face in his hands. His heart pounded in his chest like he was a teenager again and those same insecurities crashed down around him. But this was Maria and she needed his comfort. He told himself that was the only reason she was reaching out to him and he was responding.

He slicked his tongue across his bottom lip as he glanced at hers. Perfection. Her cheeks were flush and her eyes glittery. He took in a sharp breath before he pressed his lips to hers. This move would come at a price but he did it anyway.

Her lips were soft and wet and it didn't take but a second for them to part enough to give him access. He delved his tongue inside her mouth, tasting her sweet mix of coffee and the peppermint breath mint still on her tongue from when she'd popped it in her mouth on the ride home.

Austin groaned against her mouth as his muscles pulled taut with tension. How many nights had he stared at the ceiling thinking about holding her in his arms again? So many...

Maria's flat palms splayed against his chest before her fingers curled around his shoulders, pulling him toward her. In the next second, their bodies were flush and he could feel her quick heartbeat pounding against his chest, her breasts rising and falling rapidly.

There was so much heat and chemistry in the kiss that a well of need blasted through Austin faster than a lightning bolt and he wanted to get lost in the feeling, get lost with her. She gently bit his bottom lip and he thrust his tongue inside her mouth, her fingers roaming his chest. He dropped his hands, wrapping his arms around her waist, pressing her against him. It took all his self-control not to keep going.

As difficult as it was, he pulled back. She slowly opened her eyes and her gaze lifted to meet his. Her full lips were rosy against her lightly bronzed skin.

"I miss you." She said the words so low he almost couldn't hear over the rumbling sound in his own ears.

His heart thundered against his chest and his resolve melted. He dipped his head and claimed her mouth one more time.

Keep it up, O'Brien, and stopping will be even more difficult.

He pulled back enough to rest his forehead against hers.

"What happened to us?" she asked.

"Honestly? I'm still trying to figure that one out," he said. A couple of smokin' hot kisses—and they had damn sure sizzled—wouldn't solve anything.

They both stood there for the longest time, breathing in the same air.

Maybe once they figured this case out they could make some sense of their personal lives?

"We should check over those files," he said, taking a step back. "And then you can move forward with your other plans, as well."

Chapter Twelve

Maria was confused as she followed Austin to the house. Had the air between them changed? Maybe changed wasn't the best word for it. Charged was more like it—charged with so much sexual chemistry that they'd nearly ripped each other's clothes off at the edge of the yard. There was no way that she was the only one who felt the pull between them or the undeniable attraction.

He was right about one thing, though. They needed to get to the bottom of whoever was after her. With Cliff in the hospital, she was even more resolved to put the puzzle pieces together and find answers. And she needed to make that her solitary focus before someone else got hurt.

She followed Austin into the kitchen.

"Janis sent lunch over," he said.

There were still so many questions racing through her mind. She needed a minute to pull herself together. Her emotions when it came to her husband weren't something she could afford to focus on right now. He'd been smart to correct their course. Besides, that was better than thinking about how much his rejection stung after such a heated kiss. But, hey, rejection always hurt, right?

"I'll just wash up before we eat," Maria said, making a beeline for the guest bedroom.

Austin mumbled an acknowledgment, his voice still husky and she had some relief knowing that he'd been just as affected by their kisses as she had. Okay, they seemed to have impacted her more but she didn't want to overanalyze it. They'd momentarily lapsed into old habits, she thought as she slowed her pace in the hallway.

The door to baby Raina's room was closed, just like it had been last night. Maria paused in front of it, wondering if the same pale pink walls with mint green accents were inside. Had Austin cleared out the crib they'd put together?

Her stomach coiled thinking about it as her hand hovered over the knob. She remembered how excited Austin had been when the home pregnancy test had given a positive reading. Maria hadn't been so sure that she was ready. His excitement had boosted her own confidence.

Those first few months of pregnancy had been emotional and difficult. She'd been so afraid of being a bad mother that she hadn't given herself a chance to enjoy it, which would've been tough anyway early on when she spent most of her time bent over a trash can. And then, like a blinking star it was gone, and her heart had shattered. She'd been devastated and confused at how she could miss a child she'd never seen or held so much.

Because you'd wanted that little girl more than you'd wanted your next breath, a little voice in the back of her mind said.

A noise in the other room, the sound of dishes clanking, startled her. She spun to the right and stalked down the hall, not stopping until she was standing in front of the bathroom mirror. She stared at her reflection for a long moment before turning on the faucet and splashing cold water on her face.

She could do this. She could be around Austin and not wish for things she shouldn't. She could stay in this house and not allow emotion to take over. Three lies that she'd told herself over and over again a year ago.

Maria took a deep breath before forcing calm she didn't own. Solving the case was all that mattered, she told herself. Get answers and she could make the nightmares stop. Or at least one of them.

"Smells fantastic in here," she said to Austin as she took a seat at the breakfast bar.

"Janis sent over sandwiches and her special potato salad," he said, slipping onto the seat next to her. Their elbows brushed and electricity shot up her arm, still very much live from earlier.

Neither said much until the plates were clear.

"I'm on dishes." Maria made a move to get up but was stopped by Austin's hand. More inconvenient electric pulses coursed through her. She ignored them this time.

"I got it," he said.

She'd almost forgotten how self-sufficient O'Brien men were. And stubborn with an emphasis on *stubborn*, she thought with an almost smile. Arguing with him would do no good, so she handed him her plate instead.

When she really looked at him she could see the worry in his green eyes, the sorrow. She wouldn't flatter herself enough to say she was the cause. His emotions were most likely a result of losing his parents and the current situation with Denali. *Denali.* Her heart squeezed and tears brimmed. She couldn't count the number of times she'd sat on the front porch with him at her feet, wishing she could find the right words to talk about her emotions with Austin.

And his parents? Losing them sent more pain shooting through her chest. She remembered where she'd been the exact moment that she read about their so-called accident, the café on Lavaca Street. It was a Saturday. She'd gone for her morning run and then stopped off for an iced coffee and to read the paper. The headline had caused her heart to hurt so much it felt like it might explode inside her chest. Instinct had her grappling for her cell. She'd called but he didn't pick up.

Maria refocused, needing to get back on track instead of torturing herself with another blast into the past. The two of them had already determined that the unsub they were looking for was male based on his size and strength during the Lady Bird Trail attack. He had some kind of public persona that he was trying to maintain, which was most likely the reason for the indirect attacks. In fact, the first few attempts had been set up to look random or like an accident, so this guy wasn't initially trying to draw attention toward himself or her cases. Maria hadn't been close to solving any of them that she could remember—a lot of good that thought did—so this all truly felt out of the blue.

"Mind if I take a look at the pictures on your phone?"

"Be my guest," he said, motioning toward the laptop on the counter. "I already loaded them so we could examine the images on a bigger screen."

Seeing him work in the kitchen stirred more memories that she couldn't afford to indulge, so she forced her gaze off the way the muscles in his back corded and released as he stretched to reach the top shelf into the cabinet in order to put away dishes.

"See anything?" he asked. His slender hip was leaning against the bullnose edge of the granite countertop. She realized that the noise had stopped a few minutes ago and he must've been studying her ever since.

Embarrassment heated her cheeks.

"I keep thinking that everyone has something to lose on my cases. I mean, we're talking about crimes against children here. Most people who kidnap or exploit children have a lot to lose if they're discovered," she stated.

"Nothing stands out in your mind?" He folded his arms across his broad chest and her stomach flipped.

"These are the worst of what I remember working on and I get a bad feeling every time I touch any of these cases. That's why I earmarked them," she said.

"We know that we're looking for a male. Only a strong man could overpower Cliff even with the use of tear gas," Austin said.

"Our assumption that this guy has some kind of military background is probably safe," she said.

"We've already covered the fact that he'd have a lot to lose if he got caught," he stated. "Who was the last person you spoke to before this all started?"

"That would be Ansel Sanders," she said, pulling up the file with the interview. "Male, age fifty-four. I suspected him of kidnapping his niece."

"What happened?" he asked.

"The girl, six years old, was taken from her backyard by someone the family dog recognized. Mom was in the house washing dishes after lunch and the dog never barked, never alerted her to the fact that anyone was there," she said. "So, my guess is that the dog knew the unsub. Sanders had been charged with Class C misdemeanor for peeping through an eight-year-old's window roughly six months before."

"He escalated," Austin said.

"That's the typical path," she confirmed. "He'd lost his job at the glass factory where he worked the prior year and it had been the only steady job he'd had in years. He was agitated during my interview and fled town shortly after."

"Or maybe he stuck around and now he's trying to stop you before you get too close or get the evidence you need to lock him up," he said.

"He's a consideration," she conceded. "I have no way of locating him, though. And my belief is that he moved on. Possibly to another relative's house."

"Any chance he has a military background?" he asked.

"He didn't," she confirmed, returning her attention to the screen. "But he was built fairly big, strong. And he could see me as the only thing between jail and freedom. With access to the internet he could look up ways to blitz attack."

"Meaning he could fly under the radar," he said.

"Especially if he used a relative's internet account," she agreed.

"The government can't watch everyone's online activities contrary to popular belief," he stated.

"Not unless their name comes up in conjunction with an investigation. Otherwise, there just aren't enough resources," she confirmed.

Austin nodded.

"I'd been watching a bus driver along with Austin PD on this one." She shook her head. "He has a wife and kids but I think he's soliciting thirteen-year-old boys online."

"Did he spend any time in the service?" he asked.

"Yeah, he did." She rocked her head.

"Any recent developments in the case?" he asked.

"None that I remember and I'm not seeing anything marked here in the case file, either." She studied the screen. At least she had her files to help stimulate her memory. Patches were coming back.

"Which doesn't mean there aren't any. You might not have had time to enter your notes." Austin moved next to her and he stood so close that she could smell his spicy, woodsy aftershave.

"This one involves a PE teacher. He's only five-seven, though. Couldn't be him based on the size of the unsub we're looking for," she said. "I marked it in case someone else is in the background that I haven't identified yet."

"I can print out any pages you want to take a deeper look at." Austin checked the name on the screen. "Antonio Graco."

"This case bugs me." She pointed toward the next file.

Austin's lips thinned as he read the narrative. A twelve-year-old boy solicited for sexual favors by an adult male via the internet. She dealt with some of the worst crimes since they involved innocent children and they still made her stomach turn.

"I spoke to an ex-policeman as a routine part of this investigation and I can remember thinking that he wasn't telling me everything he knew. He seemed put off by my presence. At the time, I figured that he didn't like being investigated in connection with this kind of crime let alone by a woman. Some guys still have trouble with that last part. I was working alongside Round Rock PD when I came across the guy's name as a possible suspect. He'd just left the department for a security job. Said he'd had his fill of shift work and having all his decisions questioned in court," she said. "His name is Garrett Halpern."

"Sounds like a disgruntled employee or someone with a chip on his shoulder." Austin took a sip of coffee, his gaze narrowed on the screen.

"That's what I thought initially. The problem is that he managed to answer all my questions and gave me no reason to suspect him. The case went cold until more pictures showed up online," she said. "And then evidence pointed toward the original family member we suspected and the trail went cold when we couldn't make enough of a case to get a warrant. Seems like there was something else but I can't remember what for the life of me."

"Might be a good idea to circle back to the police chief and do a little digging into Halpern's background," he said.

"Vic can't get upset about that, right?" she asked, but it was a rhetorical question. The truth was that she could get into a whole lot of trouble by investigating anything that had to do with this case.

"We might be able to vet out a name or cross one off the list. It's just an informal conversation with the chief. What's the harm in that?" he asked. "And

I can't think of a safer place than the office of the chief of police."

"What about our escort?" Could they bring him in or make an excuse to lose him?

"He can follow us. Can't hurt to have an extra set of eyes wherever we go," he said.

"I'll just make a quick call to the chief and we can be on the road if you'd like to go today," she said, thinking urgency was needed.

"Let's roll," he said.

She glanced at the screen, realizing the last file hadn't been opened yet. "Hold on a sec." She clicked on the icon. "This one was interesting. A teenage prostitution ring." She scanned the suspect list that she'd put together. "Oh—also, I was in the process of investigating an airline pilot, Ronald Ferguson."

Austin jotted the name down in a notebook. "A pilot would be physically fit and I'd bet money that he'd have a military background."

"I haven't interviewed him because I was in the process of gathering evidence," she said.

"I don't see his name." Austin scanned the page. "But if he's our guy he knew about your investigation."

Maria agreed. "I haven't entered him into the system yet. I'm not even close to building a case against him."

"Okay. We'll file him in the backs of our minds as we dig a little further into Halpern," Austin said.

The drive over to Round Rock PD took less than

an hour. Chief Blair was tall, thin, with a sprinkling of gray hair at the temples. His skin was sun-worn and he had the physique of a runner. He resembled a middle-aged Richard Gere.

He remembered Maria and she introduced him to Austin before following him to his office.

"What can I do for you folks today?" Chief Blair asked, taking his seat behind his mahogany desk. The American flag stood on a pole behind his desk. He folded his hands and leaned forward. It was a courtesy question because she'd already had to inform his second-in-command of the reason for the meeting.

"Thank you for agreeing to see us, sir," Maria said.

"How could I not? You're my favorite FBI agent." He winked. It came off as a little cheesy but Maria liked the guy in general and it was important to keep good relations with the police in her region.

"We spoke on the phone about the case we'd been working on with your department," she started.

He nodded.

"I spoke to one of your officers. Actually, he'd recently left the department to take a security job with a tech company. His name is Garrett Halpern," she said.

Chief Blair nodded again and a look passed behind his gray eyes.

"What can you tell me about his background?" she asked.

"Halpern had a difficult time fitting in at the department according to my officers. He'd only been on the job for two years when he left," Chief Blair said.

"Didn't his coworkers like him?"

"There were trust issues," he confessed. "Without going into too much detail, it's safe to say that they didn't have confidence that they could count on him when they needed him."

That was a huge issue, Maria thought. And one she'd had to overcome in order to work in law enforcement. "I appreciate that you can't give away too much information on a former employee. I'm wondering if that's the real reason he left."

"I can tell you in confidence," he paused long enough to receive her acknowledgment, "that we were trying to put together a case against him. You know how difficult it is to fire a civil servant. He was insubordinate with his superiors. Didn't take criticism well when they reprimanded him. It was starting to get tense on his shift. And then he just up and quits. Problem solved. I don't mind admitting that I felt like we dodged a bullet, especially when you came around asking about him a few weeks later."

Maria went through the facts again in her mind. Halpern was a loner. He didn't fit in with the officers on a job that was all about camaraderie. "Do you know offhand if he ever served in the military?"

"As a matter of fact, he did a stint," Chief Blair said. "Most of our new hires served the country at one point in their lives."

"Do you have a valid address on him?" she asked.

"I'll have it ready before you walk out the door," he said. "But I have no idea if it's current."

"Thank you for your time, Chief," Maria said.

They collected the information and walked to the truck.

"His background matches up to the profile of someone who would use a surprise method of attack," she said once inside and back on the road. She pinched the bridge of her nose to stem a raging headache.

"He's also escalating his attacks, which makes me believe that he's becoming more desperate," Austin added. "He's trained and adept, so we'll have to be that much more cautious about dealing with him."

"I'll let Special Agent Wheeler know about the address," she said. "And then I was thinking that we could go talk to his last employer."

"You look too tired," Austin said, his gaze scanning her face. "Doing more right now is not a good idea. We've already violated doctor's orders and put your job in jeopardy. I think that's enough for one day."

Going home with Austin was a bigger threat.

Chapter Thirteen

Dallas stood on the porch of the log cabin, waiting, when they returned and Austin feared the worst about Denali. He parked outside instead of in the garage and made a beeline toward his brother. Movement came from behind Dallas's boots and Austin recognized the little dog they'd saved on their walk.

"Is that who I think it is?" Maria's voice called out from behind him. She must've bent down because the dog ran straight past Austin toward her.

Austin didn't like his brother's serious expression, so he held course.

"I wanted to stop by personally to deliver the news before you heard it somewhere else," Dallas said before Austin had a chance to speak. He feared Denali was gone and was surprised at how choked up he got thinking about losing the Chocolate Lab that had always been his sidekick and especially during this past year.

"You want to come inside?" Austin asked, and he could hear the unsteadiness in his own voice.

Dallas nodded, so they entered the log cabin with Maria and the little pooch trailing behind.

"I'll make coffee," Maria said.

"Is it Denali?" Austin managed to choke out, trying his level best to steady his voice.

"It's about the investigation into Mom's and Dad's deaths," Dallas began, motioning toward the barstools around the granite island. "I spoke to Tommy first thing this morning."

"In the hospital?"

Dallas shook his head. "No, he was released yesterday."

Austin had no idea. He felt completely out of touch with family business since the incidents with Maria but it had been more than a week, so it made sense that Tommy would be going home about now especially with how well his recovery had been going. "That's good news."

"It is," Dallas agreed. "Doc said everything's ahead of schedule with his recovery and he'll be good as new soon enough."

"That's a relief," Austin said. "Thanks for the update." He eyed his brother. "What else? Do you have news about our parents' case?" His older brother's life had been filled with a new wife and baby on top of inheriting the ranch with his five siblings. Katherine had adopted a little boy by the name of Jackson, and she and Dallas had fallen in love when he'd saved her son from an abduction attempt.

"You know Tommy," Dallas continued. "He got

bored so he had one of his deputies bring over the case file. There was something in an interview with Janis that caught his attention, and that was that Mom and Dad both had colds at the time of the murders," he said.

"I honestly don't remember, but why should that send up an alarm?" Austin asked. He hadn't gone to the art event his parents had held before the murders and had been too busy with his own responsibilities around the ranch to be in the loop.

Maria placed cups of coffee on the counter and Austin ignored the feeling of how very right it felt to have her there with him and Dallas. He chalked it up to old feelings and spending too much time together. He reminded himself of what he'd been doing the night he'd received the call about her attack, cataloging calves for the stockyard. He needed to pick up the documents from his office and bring them home to work on them as she rested. Based on how wiped out she looked, he needed to do a better job at getting her to take care of herself.

Speaking of which, his parents had a habit of powering through sickness, too.

And then it clicked why Tommy would be concerned about them having a virus. A couple of cold tablets and they said they could get through anything. "He thinks they were poisoned in connection with their cold medication?"

Dallas was already nodding. "He went back

through the crime scene photos and found a box of medicine sitting on the counter in their bathroom."

"Was it taken up as evidence?" he asked. The puppy wandered around, sniffing, and he was currently enthralled with the tip of Austin's boot.

"Not at the time. He asked permission to look over their room again, though," Dallas said. "Their room and bathroom have been cleaned regularly, so Tommy isn't making any promises."

Austin didn't have to ask whether that permission was granted to know that it was. It also meant the killer had access to his parents' bedroom. No one went in there without a key. They kept the hallway to their personal quarters locked since the main house had frequent out-of-town visitors.

"Janis already volunteered to go in for questioning," Dallas said.

"We all know that she didn't have anything to do with their murders," Austin quickly added.

"It was someone who knew their personal habits. Someone close to them, which casts suspicion close to home again," Dallas said, and Austin understood the implication.

"I'll go in for questioning," Austin said.

"I figured you'd say that. All six of us have now said the same thing," Dallas said. "Our PR firm is working on releasing a statement as soon as the news breaks. Tommy will keep a lid on it for as long as he can but he can only do so much."

"And the rest of the staff is cooperating, I'm sure," Austin said.

Dallas nodded but a look passed behind his eyes.

"I'm guessing your reaction is about Aunt Bea and Uncle Ezra?" Austin asked.

"Neither decided it would be 'necessary' to submit to further questions. They argued that they have already cooperated and that it was time the sheriff looked for the actual criminal instead of constantly annoying family members," Dallas stated.

"Seems they finally agree on something." Austin fisted his hand and dropped it onto the cold granite. The move startled the dog at his feet. He picked up the spaniel and scratched behind his ear. "Anyone claim this guy yet?"

Dallas shook his head.

"Might be good to give him a name, at least temporarily." Austin looked at Maria.

"I've always loved the name Bailey," she said.

Austin held up the pup to face him. "Is your name Bailey?"

The little dog wagged his tail and tried to lick Austin's cheek.

"Bailey it is," he said, placing the little guy on the floor. Nose to the ground, he skimmed the floor and disappeared around the breakfast bar.

"I hate to say this about family, but Uncle Ezra has been under suspicion from day one," Dallas said, getting the conversation back on track. "He's been able to use Aunt Bea as an alibi for the night of the murders but this sheds a new light on things because he could've tampered with their medicine days before."

"How long had they had the cold? Does anyone remember?" Austin asked.

"A few days, but Uncle Ezra might've only tampered with a couple of the pills figuring they'd take them sooner or later," Dallas said.

"I'm wondering if it was Dad who was the target." Austin drummed his fingers on the granite. "What would he have to gain, though?"

"I've been trying to figure that out for myself." Dallas rubbed his chin. "Tommy found correspondence between Hollister McCabe and Uncle Ezra that basically said Ezra stood to make a lot of money if he could get us to sell McCabe the back forty acres."

"McCabe always said that belonged to him. That's the piece of the property that had caused the big rift between him and Dad," Austin remembered.

"Sounds like motive to me," Maria said with an apologetic look. No one wanted to believe family could be capable of such an act.

Dallas agreed. "I think Tommy's going to have to haul him in again. Uncle Ezra has made it clear that he won't cooperate."

"Has he given any thought to the amount of bad press he could get as a result? It wouldn't look right if he didn't volunteer, as well," Austin said, his mind spinning into damage-control mode. "Might be a good angle to get Uncle Ezra to submit to further questioning."

"We'll see what happens but I thought you should know the direction that the investigation has taken." Dallas took a sip of coffee.

"Remind me where he was the night of our parents' murders." Austin folded his arms, searching his memory. So much had happened that he sure as hell didn't try to keep up with Uncle Ezra's comings and goings.

"With Aunt Bea," Dallas said. "His alibi has been ironclad."

"Can I add my two cents?" Maria asked.

"Be my guest," Austin said to Maria, curious to get her take on the situation.

"In my experience I've found that the party acting the guiltiest usually is," she said.

"That would be Uncle Ezra," Austin said. "Now that I think about it, he's been jockeying for more since Dad died."

"More what?" she asked.

"More everything. Responsibility. Power. Percentage of the land," Austin added.

"But Tommy hasn't been able to crack his alibi," Dallas said.

"Which has been strong until now considering how much he and Aunt Bea dislike each other," Maria noted. "There's another thing that strikes me as odd. Most poisonings are the MO of women."

"It's no secret that Uncle Ezra has been pointing

the finger toward someone in the house all along," Dallas said.

"Someone like *Janis*?" Maria balked. "You're joking."

"He seems pretty ready to deflect attention away from him every chance he gets," Austin said.

"Janis was the only one with access to their private quarters," Dallas stated.

"What does Joshua think about all this?" she asked.

"The same as we do. Something's not right about Uncle Ezra but no one wants to believe that he could be involved in something like this. He's a jerk and can be power hungry, but he is still family," Dallas said.

"Was he in the house anytime near the week before the murders?" Maria asked.

"As a matter of fact, he was," Dallas said. "Aunt Bea had lunch with Mom around the same time, too."

"What about other options in the house?" Maria asked. "Did, for instance, the caterer have access?"

"It's highly unlikely that they would've and the owner and her staff were accounted for all night," Dallas said. "Plus, we've been using the same company for more years than I can count. And no one in the small company had anything to gain from their murders. Uncle Ezra, on the other hand did, but then he'd still have to convince the six of us to do what Dad wouldn't. The caterers stood to lose one of their biggest customers without Mom and Dad."

"Donors? Artists?" she continued.

Dallas shook his head. "Neither had access or a good reason. Mom and Dad did nothing but help the art community. Again, their deaths would hurt more than help. As far as donors go, nothing's come up in anyone's background so far. The only person in the world who would like to see Dad dead is Hollister McCabe and he's in jail."

Maria nodded that she was aware of the rift between the McCabes and O'Briens.

Until his brother Ryder got involved in a relationship with Faith McCabe, the O'Briens would've written all the family members off. She'd proved to be on their side and just as disgusted by her father who was no good, as evidenced by him turning his back on the half brother she had been sneaking around to help.

"What about other employees?" Maria asked.

"Cynthia Stoker, our event planner, was in the kitchen with Janis for most of the night," Dallas said. "When she wasn't with Janis, she was mingling with party guests, making sure everyone had a good time."

"Cynthia helped plan our wedding," Maria said with a small smile that fisted Austin's heart.

"Stacy came on board after Mom and Dad were gone," Austin said.

"Who's she?" Was there a note of jealousy in Maria's voice? She picked up Bailey and nuzzled him to her chest.

"Someone we hired a few months ago to work as Janis's assistant," Austin said. "Someone we can trust."

"And that's it?" she asked.

"The box of cold medicine might give Tommy a clue as to who did this," Dallas offered.

"Think he can lift a set of prints off it?" Austin asked Maria.

"It's possible. There might be a better chance of getting prints from the room, from metal or glass, but a good lab might be able to pick something up from the box even though a lot of time has passed," Maria added. "How well do you know Stacy?"

"Her previous employer was killed on an assignment helping me." Dallas pushed off his barstool and stood. He drained his mug before setting it down on the counter. "That's all I have for now. We'll know more once they talk to Uncle Ezra. Tommy wants to bring in someone from a different agency to interview him."

"Makes sense to get someone with a fresh perspective," Maria said. "I'm happy to watch the interview, if you'd like."

"I'll let Tommy know," Dallas said. "I realize your plate is full right now, so we appreciate the offer."

Maria nodded and smiled.

"In the meantime, I thought you should know about Denali," Dallas said. "He's comfortable but the vet doesn't have high hopes right now. He said we should tell everyone to stop by and see him. His breathing is labored and his gums are a bright red color, which the vet says isn't a good sign at this point. She'd hoped that he would have progressed by now but with his advanced age…"

"I'm sorry to hear it. He's a good dog," Maria said. Her voice was thick with emotion. "It's a shame someone would do this to him."

"Do you know who was on the property at the time he was poisoned?" Austin asked, fighting back the well of emotion threatening to bust through his walls.

"The usual. Staff. Family. No one out of the ordinary because we've kept security tight. Uncle Ezra had asked for another meeting," Dallas supplied.

Dallas let out the kind of sharp breath that expressed how deeply his frustration ran. They needed to catch a break in this case. Running a ranch wasn't like other businesses. Walking away even for a day wasn't a serious consideration and dark circles cradled Dallas's eyes from burning the candle at both ends. Austin was all too familiar with that routine and guilt stabbed at him for leaving his brothers to pick up his slack lately.

"Go home to your wife and kid," Austin said, patting his brother on the back. "I'll bring the paperwork home and keep up with logging calves at night. Speaking of which, did the vet get any closer to an answer with what's going on with them?"

Dallas shook his head. "The only news so far is that they don't seem to be getting worse."

The family couldn't seem to catch a break lately.

"And we haven't lost any, yet. And that's the only good news I have for you today," Dallas said.

"I'll take what I can get." Austin followed his brother to the door. Dallas was being cautious but the calves stabilizing was a step in the right direction.

Dallas glanced down at Bailey. "You want me to take him up to the main house?"

Austin studied Maria as she cuddled the mutt. "We can drop him by in the morning. Let him settle here overnight."

Dallas nodded. "Nice to see you again, Maria. I hope you don't mind my saying this but it's good to have you home."

It was a big statement and Austin half expected Maria to balk. She didn't. Instead, she said, "Good to be here."

Dallas made a move to turn toward the door but Maria held up a hand to stop him.

"I know about the deal with Uncle Ezra and Hollister McCabe but it's sketchy that would work out even with your dad out of the equation. Was there anything else that you can think of that Uncle Ezra might gain if he didn't get a bigger inheritance?" she asked.

"That's a tough question. I see what you're getting at, establishing motive," Dallas replied. "He and Aunt Bea inherited their portion of the business years ago."

"And they received nothing extra in the will?" she asked.

Dallas and Austin both shook their heads in unison.

"That would make the case more clear-cut, wouldn't it?" Austin asked.

"But he's been pressuring you guys for more responsibility and more power ever since?" she asked.

Again, they nodded.

"So, the trick is figuring out if he and your father were in a fight before the so-called 'accident.'" She brought her coffee mug to her lips but didn't take a sip. "Or if Uncle Ezra had something directly to gain from your father's death. But then, he might've just thought it would be easier to get what he wanted from the six of you with your father out of the picture."

"Dad never said anything about his brother, but then he wasn't the type to bad-mouth someone. If Dad had a problem with you, you knew it but the world didn't," Austin stated.

"He was a good man," Maria agreed.

Everyone stayed quiet for a few seconds that stretched on.

Dallas gave his brother a hug. "I'll let you know the second I hear anything more from Tommy."

Chapter Fourteen

Thinking about his parents' murders had soured Austin's mood. But even that dissolved the second he saw Denali lying on the table with tubes sticking out of him. Janis was there, a ball of tissues in hand, red-rimmed eyes and nose. And there was a blanket over most of Denali's body. Austin wanted to come alone, to spend time one-on-one with Denali.

"I'll leave you two alone," she said in a church-quiet voice as she pushed up to her feet and gazed down at the Lab.

"How is he?" Austin asked quietly, rounding the table to where Denali faced.

Janis's lips compressed into a frown as she shook her head, and she seemed too choked up to speak. Her gaze intensified on the white tile floor as she hurried past.

Austin took in a sharp breath. He focused on being grateful that Denali was surrounded by so much love. He already knew that the Lab had some-one constantly by his side since being found. Fitting, he thought, since Denali had always been a steady and loyal companion to so many for his fourteen years of life. It would be right for him... No— Austin couldn't even think about Denali being gone. He *had* to pull through.

The round stool was cold as Austin took a seat next to Denali's head. The sweet dog's breathing was labored. Denali whined in his sleep and his right leg involuntarily jerked. Austin couldn't choke back the tears welling. He'd shed them only one other time in his life, when he'd found out about his parents. He thought tears would've flowed when he'd lost Raina. They hadn't. He'd been too busy stuffing down his emotions and trying to figure out how to help his wife.

Denali panted and whined.

"You're okay, boy." Austin scratched that favorite spot behind his buddy's ear as more tears rolled down his cheeks.

Denali opened his eyes and immediately wagged his tail. He made a move to get up but it seemed to take great effort. Austin threw his arm around the dog's neck to calm him.

"Stay right here, buddy," Austin said in a low, quiet voice.

The dog stilled except for his tail, which wagged in double time.

All Austin could think about was how Denali had stayed by his side for the past year as though he'd had a sixth sense, as though he'd been keeping vigilant watch. Austin had worked late into the night and there'd been Denali right by his side.

Denali took in a shaky breath and Austin lost it.

"Oh, boy, don't go," was all Austin could manage through the barrage. The pain of the past year compounded by losing his daughter, his wife and then both his parents bore down on him as he held his companion in his arms, willing him to live.

"Don't leave me."

BY THE TIME Austin returned home, he had a stack of papers and his laptop tucked underneath his arm. Leaving Denali was one of the hardest things he'd ever done. The vet had reassured Austin ten times over that the Lab was in stable condition and Austin wasn't the only one wanting to hold a bedside vigil for the animal. He needed to give his brothers time to be with their dog and try to make peace with the thought of losing him. Austin was not in a place where he could accept that outcome. Convincing himself that Denali would be fine was the only reason he could walk out that door.

It was two o'clock in the morning when he parked in front of his cabin. There was a soft light on in the living room.

He toed off his boots at the front door, glancing around for Maria. He half expected her to be sitting there, waiting. She wasn't. She was most likely sleeping but he tiptoed toward the guest room anyway for reasons he couldn't explain. Maybe he needed a reminder that she was still there after spending time with Denali. There was something reassuring about her presence on the ranch, in their home, that Austin shouldn't allow himself to get too comfortable with.

For now, he had no plans to analyze it. He was running on raw emotion.

The door to Raina's room was cracked open and a soft light peeked through into the hallway.

Austin froze.

Maria wouldn't even go near that hallway after she'd lost the baby…and it took his brain a minute to process the notion that she was in there right now. He forced his feet to move toward the light, stopping at the door. He told himself that all he needed was a quick visual to make sure that Maria was okay. He'd expected to hear crying coming from the room, but then, like him, he hadn't seen Maria cry since losing their little girl.

"Austin?" Maria's voice was raw.

He suddenly felt awkward standing there, like he was intruding on a very private moment.

"I saw the light on," was all he managed to say.

"Do you remember this picture?" she asked, so he opened the door and stepped inside.

All the memories flooded him even though he'd been inside the room a couple of times since Maria had left as though he might find some clue as to what had made her shut down and call quits on their marriage.

He walked over to where she sat on the floor next

to the glider in the corner. The pink patchwork quilt his mother had made was draped over her legs as she stared at the baby book in her hands.

The picture was of her, fresh-faced and holding up the stick that revealed she was pregnant, beaming. Her long dark hair was pulled back in a ponytail and she wore a light blue tank top. He remembered that she'd just returned from her morning jog and had said that she'd stopped off to throw up twice. A phone call to her friend had prompted her to swing by the drugstore and buy a pregnancy test.

They'd had no idea what life was about to hand them, he thought as he stared at their wide smiles.

He was also reminded at how easy it had been to fall in love with her even though she'd seemed determined not to give in. He'd won her over with persistence, a well-timed punch line and apparently his "intense" green eyes, as she'd put it.

She closed her hand on his and tugged him down next to her. Austin complied but his heart cautioned this wasn't a good idea. His emotions were too raw and he needed to be strong for her.

"I'm sorry," she said quietly.

"It wasn't your fault," he stated.

"I was hoping that she'd look like you."

TEARS STREAMED DOWN Maria's cheeks. Austin was there, sitting next to her, and before she could debate her actions she climbed onto his lap and pressed her lips to his. His arms looped around her waist and his touch was so tender it robbed her of breath. She took in the scent of him, masculine and spicy. She was seeking refuge, comfort, and his touch was more than reassuring as he splayed his strong hand on her back. Sensual shivers raced up her spine and warmth pooled low in her belly.

Emotions came crashing down around her. A mix of longing, regret and an ache she had tried so hard to fill since walking out the door last year.

"I miss this…*you*." His words were so low she almost thought she'd imagined hearing them, thinking they were words she'd wanted to hear far too long. And yet, she'd been the one to walk away, not him. Everything was her fault.

The thought was sobering, so she pushed up, apologized and hurried out of the room before he could see the shame on her face.

"Don't do this," he said, following closely behind.

She'd felt his presence even before he spoke. There was something magnetic about Austin. So much so that she sensed him whenever he was near. Maria stopped at the granite breakfast bar and whirled around. "What?"

"Don't shut me out this time," he said, and there was so much hurt he was masking with his deep timbre. "Just tell me what I did to push you away."

How could she look him in the eye and tell him that everything was her fault?

"Nothing." She turned away from him but felt his

firm grip on her arm, stopping her from running in the opposite direction.

"We never talked about it, about what went wrong between us," he said.

"I already said." Maria pulled her arm free and thought long and hard about their situation. She had no right to ask for what she wanted, needed from Austin. And yet, she was about to do just that anyway.

Spinning around to face him, she slicked her tongue across her bottom lip and took a tentative step toward him. Afraid to look into his eyes, afraid of the hurt that was all her fault, she focused on his chest. Austin was quiet strength personified.

"Kiss me again," she said, and then held her breath, waiting for his response.

It came quickly. One step was all it took for him to be nose to nose with her, mouth to mouth.

She pressed up on her tiptoes and tangled her arms around his neck as her breasts thrust forward against his muscled chest. Her nipple beaded as his thumb grazed over it and he groaned.

In the next second, his hands were on her hips, lifting her until she perched on the barstool. He stepped into the V of her thighs and she wrapped her long legs around his midsection as his lips pressed hard to hers and his tongue slid inside her mouth. This time, the groan he released was primal, guttural. She felt it rumble from somewhere deep inside his chest. Warmth pooled between her thighs as his erection pressed against her sweet heat. Need welled up so quickly that her head was spinning and she was getting lost in the feeling of being with the man she missed, her Texas rancher.

Two thin strips of denim were all that kept them apart and she was very aware of the barrier.

Her body strained for sweet release—release only the man she loved could give her.

The man she loved?

Yeah, she still loved Austin. But her love was toxic, like drinking contaminated water, and it was only a matter of time before she hurt him again if she let this go any further. He seemed to sense her hesitation because he pulled back.

His pupils were dilated and he had an almost animallike need in his expression.

"I want to say this is a good idea," she said, her breath coming out in rasps.

"If we make love it'll change things between us," he said, and his voice was low and husky, like whiskey poured over crackling ice.

"That's true," she said, trying to steady her rapid pulse.

"Which might not be a bad thing," he said.

If they could handle it, she wanted to add, but didn't. The truth was that she would only cause more heartache for Austin. She could see that clearly now.

"Your hesitation tells me that we need to get a handle on this," he said without budging. He pressed his forehead to hers and mumbled something that sounded like *Not the right timing*.

He was right, though. It wasn't. And it would never be for her. She had too many demons and, unlike a sinking swimmer, she had no plans to drag him down along with her as she drowned.

THERE WAS SOMETHING cleansing about having a good cry. Most of the time Maria prayed for the sweet release of tears and they never came. All she'd had were dry sockets. Last night felt as though someone had released the dam. She'd climbed into bed, pulled the covers up and sobbed.

This morning, she woke before the sun, feeling better than she could remember.

Maria stretched out her arms and legs before going through her usual morning routine of brushing her teeth and washing her face. She threw her hair in a ponytail and put on workout clothes. Going for a run sounded amazing and she could get away with one safely on the O'Brien property.

After breakfast, she'd check in with Vic and see if any of the leads she gave him yesterday had panned out.

The light was on inside the master bedroom. Austin was most likely working. She hated to interrupt him but she had to let him know her plans. Walking softly, she eased toward the cracked door. Austin was at the desk in the corner—all he had to do was look left and he'd see her. Bailey was at his feet, snoring.

She knocked softly.

Austin glanced up and she knew instantly that he hadn't slept.

"Come in," he said, rubbing his eyes.

She'd rather stay in the hallway, so she opened the door wider and brought her arm up to rest on the doorjamb.

"I was just about to head out for a run," she said, admiring his good looks and strong body as he stretched. He wore jeans and his chest was bare.

"You want company?" he asked, biting back a yawn.

"Looks like you could use caffeine," she said.

"I won't deny that, but exercise might kick my brain in gear again. I had to reenter the last number six times before I got it right," he said with the same smile that had been so good at melting her resolve.

Bailey's tail started wagging before he made a move to get up.

"He needs to go out anyway," Austin said. He stood there, shirtless with his jeans low on his hips, and Maria couldn't help but stare at his muscled body. Austin's stomach was ripped and she could see every bit of his definition as he moved toward the bed and pulled a black V-neck T-shirt over his head. Her gaze traveled down with the hem to a perfectly toned stomach and the patch of dark hair below his belly button.

It should feel awkward standing there practically gawking at him, but there had always been something so right about being around Austin. Something so casual about seeing him walk around wearing next to nothing, with only a towel secured around his waist. Being naked was the most natural thing in the world…

Until he started unbuttoning his jeans and then awareness skittered across her skin, awakening her nerve endings and making her keenly aware that he was all man and she was a woman. It was primal as all hell but she couldn't control that any more than she could stop the sun from rising. It was imprinted in nature and her primal instincts made her very aware of the virile male presence in the room.

Another few seconds later and his jeans were piled on the wood floor. Was it getting hot outside already? She sure felt the heat inside the room. Her mouth went dry and her palms sweaty as he slipped into basketball shorts.

Thankfully, he hadn't made eye contact yet because when he looked up, a lightning bolt of need coursed through her, electric and energetic.

Maria tried to swallow to ease the dryness in her throat and only succeeded in making a strained angry-frog sound.

Austin's lips upturned in a smile—the one that had been so good at seducing her—and it might've been arrogant but it was sexy as hell, too.

"I'll just put on a pot of coffee for when we get back," she managed to squeak out as she backed away from the door slowly. Memories of their naked bodies entangled in those sheets assaulted her, wreaking havoc on her breathing.

She needed to get out of there…*now*.

Chapter Fifteen

Austin shook his head and laughed. Good that he thought it was funny because it was taking all of Maria's strength to walk out of that room and not… *complicate* matters further with a round of the most amazing sex she knew she'd ever have. Mainly because sex with Austin had been the best of her life and she had no doubt that his…*skills*…were sharp as ever. He might've had an uncharacteristic moment or two of soft emotions last night but he was all alpha and male and virile in bed. But there was so much more than physical appeal when it came to Austin. He was sharp and had the most penetrating eyes.

He was the only person she'd ever felt like she could truly let her guard down around and be herself, she thought as she poured water into the carafe and then transferred it into the machine. He'd believed her to be confident and never seemed to see her weaknesses. She had them. Plenty of them, she thought.

Maria knew the second he entered the room and

not because Bailey's nails clicked on the tile floor-
ing in the kitchen. Her arms goose bumped the second she felt his presence.

He came up behind her, close enough that she
could hear him breathing, and ran a finger along the
base of her neck. She wanted to lean back against
him and get lost in the feeling. And then his hand
came up to her waist. She sucked in a burst of air the
second he touched her, trying to absorb the electricity pinging through her.

"Are we okay?" he asked.

"Yeah," she said, and then almost lost it when he
took a step closer and pressed his lips to the nape
of her neck.

"Last night was hell," he admitted, splaying his
long fingers flat against her stomach.

A thousand butterflies released, fluttering wildly.

"I couldn't sleep after being in her room together,"
he added, and she could feel his lips move against
her skin when he spoke.

Sensual shivers raced down her back and she was
so very aware of Austin.

"How's Denali?" she asked, needing to reframe
the conversation or fall down that same rabbit hole
of desire again. Now that many of her memories
had returned she knew that Austin would never for-
give her. And even if forgiveness was possible, he
deserved more than she could give him. She would
always be damaged, broken. And she would always
leave a trail of destruction in her wake.

Austin's finger trailed down the line of her neck, her shoulder, her arm, threatening to erase all her concerns. They'd all but disappeared for the moment, at least, as he stroked her collarbone. She turned to face him and accidently ushered in more of his scent, which wasn't a good idea given how much her body reacted to his presence. His dark green eyes were even more striking, like they always became when he was intensely emotional. And she'd forgotten just how telling they could be. She wished there was something that she could say to take away at least some of his torment.

"He'll be okay, won't he?" she asked, not bothering to mask her fear.

"The vet can't say for sure. I'd like to stop by again this morning," he said, and his voice was husky.

"I'd like that, as well. If I can come, that is," she said, figuring she shouldn't take for granted that he'd want her there.

Austin nodded and she took that as a positive sign.

Capitalizing on his goodwill, she linked their fingers and pressed up to her tiptoes. His muscles corded and his face wore the expression he had when he was trying to figure out if something was a good idea.

Apparently, he decided this wasn't because he took a step back and released her fingers. "I can't, Maria. It's easy to slip into old patterns when you're here, standing in our kitchen, and I can't deny that it feels a certain sense of right that's been missing the past year. But it seemed pretty damn easy for you to start up a relationship with someone else."

"What's that supposed to mean?" she shot back. "Do you really think that I could let things get out of control with you if I'd been in a relationship with someone else?"

"That's what you're worried about?" He folded his arms across his chest.

"Why don't you just spell it out for me, Austin?"

"You want a road map? Fine. How long did it take for you to run to him after you left me?" His words were full of venom now.

"Is that what you think?" she asked, and this time she let him know just how directly he'd scored.

"What am I supposed to believe? I find out from Tommy that you're engaged to another man at the same time you have divorce papers sent to me," he said.

"I was not...*have not been* planning a wedding," she said, angry tears blurring her vision. "And especially not with someone I went out with a couple of times."

"Then I'm confused," he said.

"Damn right you are," she shot back, storming out of the kitchen. By the time she'd stalked into the guest room she realized how badly she needed caffeine. If it didn't mean facing down Austin while crying almost uncontrollably she'd march right back in there and get it. Maria had been holding in tears for the past year, hell, for most of her life. And suddenly she was a faucet. The problem was that she'd let her guard down. Was that the absolute smartest thing she could've done? Probably not. And especially not after going into Raina's room. That brought all kinds of unexpected emotions bubbling to the surface.

And, you know what? Now that she really thought about it Austin didn't get to stir up that pot and walk away.

No, sir. She was marching right back into the kitchen and giving him a piece of her mind. Right after she wiped all those tears off her face.

Maria took a minute to pull herself together before pushing off the bed. A deep breath later and she was ready. She stalked toward the door, opened it so hard that it smacked against the rubber doorstop and ran almost smack into Austin's chest. Damn, he was tall standing this close.

"Don't say it," he said, holding up a hand to stop her from speaking.

Well, guess what? He didn't have magic hands. Okay, she took that back. His hands could be pretty existential but that wasn't the point she was trying to make here and thinking that only made her more flustered.

"You don't get to shush me," she fired at him.

His incredulous look made her crack a smile despite herself.

"By all means," he said with a hint of a smirk curling the right corner of his mouth.

Trying to fight with him had never worked as

planned. They'd dissolved into laughter at the most inappropriate moment and the fight could never gain any steam.

Maria held on to her anger this time, stuffing down the urge to crack a wider smile.

"First of all, I'm not and have never been engaged to Mitch DeCarlo," she said, noticing how Austin cringed at the sound of his name.

"Noted." There was no hint of amusement on his face now. "Again, I have to ask if he knows that."

"Yeah, he does now," she said, poking a finger in Austin's chest. It was like stabbing at a brick wall. "We went on a couple of dates." She added, "Recently," when his lips thinned.

"How recently?"

"In the past month," she clarified.

"Then why does the man think he's marrying you?" Austin asked. "And why is he going around telling people that you're engaged?"

She shrugged. "I seriously have no idea how he made the leap from me accepting a date after he'd been bugging me for months to us getting married after going out a handful of times." Austin started to object but she cut him off. "A handful, as in four dates."

His facade didn't crack as he stood there, arms folded over his broad chest.

"The only reason I ever went out with him was because I thought it was time to try to get over my feelings for you," she fired. "But don't get all crazy on me thinking that I can never be with another man because I most certainly can now that I see how much you hate me."

"Hate you?" he parroted.

"That's what I said." She regretted oversharing the minute his granite expression changed. Anger was so much easier to deal with than pain.

"What makes you think that?" he asked, his gaze wide and his green eyes infuriatingly beautiful.

He'd laugh if he heard her describe him in that way, but *beautiful* really suited him, both inside and out. And especially out, her body cried, standing this close. A stubborn little voice in the back of her head added that he was intelligent, too. But this wasn't the time for a laundry list of Austin O'Brien's good qualities.

His back teeth clenched and she decided to gear up for the fight. Part of her panicked and wanted to run, to get out of there and get fresh air. But another part, a part she'd ignored in the past, forced her feet to stick to the carpet in the hallway.

It was so difficult to stand there and not reach out to touch him. Finding the right words to explain her actions was so damn hard.

But they needed to talk. And she was ready to have the conversation they'd needed to have for the past year.

"Ring of Fire" belted out of Austin's pocket, interrupting the moment happening between him and

Maria. He cursed under his breath because he was about to show her how much he actually loved her. Loved?

Yeah, he reasoned, as he fished out his cell and answered the call from Dallas.

"What's up?" Austin asked.

"Thought you should know that I'm on my way and I have a surprise for you," his brother said. "You're still home, right?"

"Yeah," he said.

"And you're planning to stick around?" Dallas continued.

"Sure." Austin shoved his free hand in his pocket and took a few steps away from Maria. He needed to cool his jets anyway. This was as good a reason to take a break as any.

"I'm almost there and there's something you need to see for yourself," Dallas said and the excitement in his voice made Austin curious.

"I'm guessing that I don't get to know what this is about?" he asked, trying to figure out how to handle his heightened emotions.

"Nope," came the response.

"Then, I'll wait here for you," he said, figuring a few deep breaths would go a long way toward lowering his blood pressure.

"Ten minutes," Dallas stated, and he sounded particularly pleased with himself, which was good for him because Austin was all kinds of confused.

Dallas disconnected the call before Austin had

a chance to pump him for information. And by the time he whirled back around to talk to Maria she'd disappeared. He hadn't heard her footsteps but he assumed she'd gone to her room. All Austin could think to do was turn on the coffee maker.

He was no good at waiting, he thought, as he scraped the heel of his shoe across the wood floor as time seemed to drip by. He was reminded of that old saying about a watched pot never boiling. His mom had said that a thousand times over the years when one of the boys had grown impatient. Little good it was doing him now.

After that intense conversation with Maria, he felt like he could break through the wall that had been impenetrable. Part of him wanted to stalk down the hall and tell her what was really on his mind. He needed to relax before having the conversation they both needed to have and finally seemed ready for. Besides, he didn't want to get into it with her when Dallas could show up at any minute.

Hearing gravel crunch underneath Dallas's pickup truck broke the tension. Austin set his mug down and shouted to let Maria know his brother was there. Austin had no idea what Dallas had up his sleeve but he could use good news for a change.

Austin made a beeline for the front door as he heard footsteps coming toward him from the hallway.

"I'm sorry I disappeared on you in the middle of our…"

"Fight." He finished her sentence.

"Yeah. That." Maria's face twisted and he figured that she was about to apologize.

"We can't work anything out if you keep on walking away. You know that, right?" he asked with more compassion than anger. She looked as miserable as he felt.

"I do."

Those were two words he could work with. Austin offered a smile. "Good. Then we'll finish our conversation when my brother leaves."

She locked onto his gaze and pursed her lips. "Agreed."

Hope took seed in Austin's chest. Hearing that she wasn't and hadn't been in a relationship with another man sent relief rippling through him. He wondered how things got so confused between them. There'd been so many assumptions and miscommunications. If he and Maria could open the lines of communication they had a chance at repairing their relationship. His feelings for her hadn't dimmed in the past year and that's one of the many reasons he knew they were the real deal. Given a chance, they might be able to flourish again. But better this time. Because they both seemed ready to open up to the possibility of more.

"Let's see what's so important to Dallas," he said, linking their fingers before leading her to the door.

Austin's heart nearly exploded with happiness when he opened the screen door and stepped onto the porch. He immediately dropped to his knees as the hundred pound Lab ambled up the stairs.

The minute Denali made eye contact, his tail went crazy.

"He perked up last night not long after you left," Dallas said. Austin could hear the smile in his brother's voice. "Vet wants to know what kind of magic you're carrying around because she could use it for her other patients."

Wrapping his arms around the dog's neck, Austin was overwhelmed with love.

"You did it," he said quietly. "You stayed."

Maria was by Austin's side. Bailey was there, too. And the little dog was nuzzling his snout against the big Chocolate Lab as the two got acquainted.

"I thought he might cheer you up," Dallas said with a broad smile.

"Seeing this guy up and around is more than I could've hoped for," Austin said, holding to himself that being with Maria was right up there with the best moments of his life.

"Well, I can make your day even better. The calves are improving."

Before Austin could respond his brother's cell buzzed and he answered quickly after a cursory glance at the screen.

"Is that right?" Dallas said after a few seconds. After asking his caller to hold he said to Austin, "Gideon said Uncle Ezra and Aunt Bea are at the gate, demanding to speak to us."

"Good. I'll let Tommy know," Austin said before pulling his cell out of his back pocket. He sent a text and received an immediate response that Tommy would head over.

"Okay," Dallas said into the phone before ending the call.

"What's got him riled up today?" Austin asked.

"Tommy got a warrant and searched his place this morning," Dallas said.

"This should be interesting." Austin glanced at Maria and then refocused on Denali, thinking that even through the craziness he had a lot to be grateful for.

Chapter Sixteen

Rapid knocks at the front door fired off like a police raid. Austin set down his coffee cup and moved toward the racket.

He'd barely opened the door when Uncle Ezra pushed past him.

"Morning, Aunt Bea," Austin said as she nodded, head down, following closely behind her brother. Austin noted the odd behavior and moved on.

He cocked an eyebrow at Gideon, who trailed them both. Tommy was already barreling down the drive toward the house so Austin left the door open. The dogs were out back with Maria.

"Morning," he said to Tommy as he took the porch steps at a good clip. "Shouldn't you be resting or still at the hospital?"

"Not enough excitement there. Besides, I've been on my back too long already." Tommy's skin was pale and he looked winded but he seemed to force a smile anyway. "I see they're already here."

"Just arrived." Austin shot Tommy a look before

leading him into the kitchen where voices were already at shouting levels. "All right. Everyone calm down."

Uncle Ezra took that as his cue to raise his voice. His face was already red and he'd end up having a heart attack if he kept at it.

Austin picked up a metal spoon and banged it on a pot. "I said quiet."

It worked. The room fell silent.

"One at a time," Austin said before looking at Uncle Ezra. "What's going on?"

Uncle Ezra's face scrunched up like a pickled prune as he focused on Tommy. "*He's* my problem. When is he going to leave this family alone and find the man who killed my brother and sister-in-law?"

Tommy blew out a sharp breath. "I'm sorry if my investigation inconveniences you, but I go where the evidence leads."

Those words were a forest fire lit at Uncle Ezra's feet that quickly consumed him in anger. "If that were true then you'd be following a different trail. So far, all you've done is question me and that's why I brought Bea here. She'll back me up and tell you for the hundredth time that I was *with her*."

Aunt Bea's hands were twisted together as she nodded. She seemed extra nervous and a little panicked as Maria entered the room with the dogs. Denali immediately whimpered as he tried to turn tail and run.

Didn't that flare up all Austin's warning bells? He instinctively stepped in between Aunt Bea and the dog.

"What's going on?" Austin asked his aunt, watching her carefully.

"I just wish they'd find the horrible man who did this." Her gaze fixed on a spot behind Austin. He turned in time to see Denali moving toward the door. The Lab whimpered, which was totally uncharacteristic of him.

Maria studied the dog and then Aunt Bea.

"You're right, Aunt Bea, I wish Tommy would find the man who did this." She took a threatening step toward Aunt Bea. Austin caught on and anger nearly consumed him.

His aunt inched backward toward the front door as her hand-twisting intensified. She could no longer make eye contact and Austin remembered what Maria had said. The person acting guilty usually is.

"But that's been the problem all along, hasn't it? Tommy's been looking for a man when he should've been searching for a woman," Maria said, and guilt flashed across Aunt Bea's face.

And then chaos erupted as Aunt Bea made a run for it and Uncle Ezra came up with a knife.

"Step back," he said, waving the blade in the air. "Do it now!"

"Why'd you do it?" Austin asked.

"I made a deal with McCabe for a parcel of land

and your father was so stubborn. He wouldn't give an inch and he said horrible things to me and your uncle. So, I decided we should take matters into our own hands. My daughter lost her job and times have been tight for her. I wanted to help and when I proposed the idea to your father about the land deal he threatened to cut me out completely and take away what I already had." Her eyes were wild. "I couldn't let him do that, so I told Ezra what we needed to do and he agreed."

Aunt Bea made a move for the door when Austin dived at Uncle Ezra and landed headfirst into the man's knees in a football tackle. The knife sliced Austin's shoulder before he wrangled the blade out of Uncle Ezra's hands. In the next second, Gideon, Dallas and Tommy were in the fray. Austin eased his weight off the older man as Tommy spun Uncle Ezra facedown and zip-cuffed his wrists behind his back.

Maria had already taken care of Aunt Bea. By the time Austin stood up again, Maria's knee was lodged in Aunt Bea's back and she was eating carpet.

"I hope they throw away the key when they lock you up," Maria said.

Tommy stalked over to Aunt Bea and cuffed her next as Austin moved to Denali's side.

"It's okay, boy," he soothed. "She can't hurt you again, buddy."

Denali leaned his body against Austin, as though for comfort.

"I know. She hurt you before but it's over," he said, and that covered so much more than just for Denali. His parents would finally receive justice for their murders. It had taken all of Austin's self-control not to snap Uncle Ezra's neck when he'd been on top of him. He could've done it so easily. Death was too simple for his uncle. Ezra needed to suffer behind bars for the rest of his miserable life. As for Bea, she would get everything she had coming to her.

Dallas immediately tracked over to Austin, dropped to his knees and embraced both him and Denali in the same hug. Maria's arms tangled in as well and he could hear her sob. Not tears of sadness, but the sound of healing tears.

It was done. His parents could finally rest in peace.

"I'll call the others for a meeting and fill them in on what happened here today," Dallas finally said, standing when the evil had been removed from Austin's house. Gideon helped Tommy stuff them in the back of his SUV. They were going where they belonged.

"We have answers," Austin said. "And we'll get justice."

Dallas agreed, and then he left, too.

Austin and Maria were on the floor with the dogs curled next to them. Bailey and Denali had become fast friends. He and Maria held on to each other and she felt so damn right in his arms.

When Denali and Bailey fell asleep, Austin slowly eased away from them, taking Maria with him. Neither spoke as though words might shatter the sacred quiet around them. They didn't need words to communicate how much they needed each other in that moment.

And so, Austin linked their fingers and took his wife to bed.

She kissed him first. His hands went to the hem of her shirt and she helped him lift it off her, her breasts rising and falling with movement. Austin ran his finger along the trim of her bra. Her chest rose and fell rapidly, matching his own breathing.

He palmed her breast and a blast of need rocketed through him when her nipple beaded against his skin.

All he could do was close his mouth over hers and slide his tongue inside her mouth again.

Her fingers worked the snap on her bra before helping him out of his shirt, and the feeling of her smooth, creamy skin against his chest corded his muscles. A second later and his running shorts were on the floor. It didn't take but a few more for hers to join his. And then she dropped her silk-and-lace panties as he slipped out of his boxers.

She slipped the rubber band off her ponytail and her hair fell around her shoulders, brushing his sensitized skin. Awareness plowed through him and his erection pulsed. He had to slow things down because when she palmed his shaft he nearly exploded.

So he picked her up, her long legs wrapped around his midsection, and he drove his tip inside her slick heat. She was wet and ready for him, so he thrust a little deeper, making sure he wasn't hurting her with his length. Her sexy little moan, her arms around his neck and her hands tunneled inside his hair nearly sent him to the brink. But he wanted this to last. He wanted to take it slow and pleasure her until she begged for release.

"I need you, Austin," came out in between breaths as she rocked her hips back and forth, working his shaft until he almost came first.

"My beautiful Maria," was all he could say in response as her muscles clenched around him.

He moved to the bed without breaking their rhythm and she moaned her pleasure as he drove deeper inside her. Her legs were high around him and he turned to plant a kiss on one before putting more of his weight on top of her and taking her mouth again.

Their pace was dizzying and frantic and…

He groaned in order to hold back. He wanted her to reach the abyss first and her frantic pace said she was on the brink.

He gripped her waist, letting her take the lead as she ground against him and sent pleasure rocketing through him.

She looked up at him with wild, sexy eyes, her hair in a tangle on the sheets, and that one look nearly obliterated him as he felt her muscles constrict and release around his shaft.

Her pacing slowed as she floated back to earth and smiled at him.

"Your turn," was all she said before she scooted out from underneath him, breaking contact.

He frowned until he realized what she was doing when she flipped him onto his back and straddled him. With two hands, he grabbed her sweet round bottom as she lowered down on him, taking him inside her.

With her hands firmly planted on his chest, she bent over and kissed him before rocking his world. The rhythm she set was fast and hard and intense. He gripped her waist and drove her sex against his in a dizzying pace until he was driven to the edge.

He detonated with her in the ring of fire, engulfing them.

By the time they reached release they were both heaving for air. She dropped down beside him on the bed, drained.

When she looked at him, all they could do was laugh. That was the best damn sex of Austin's life.

"I miss everything about you," he said.

She curled over to face him and he wrapped his arm around her, pulling her closer.

"I miss you, too, Austin." Her big doe eyes were still glittery and her smile was like watching a bird take flight. "I miss all of it."

"The question is…what should we do about it?" Austin pulled her down for a kiss.

"What we should've done a year ago," she said, "talk."

AUSTIN STIRRED AND blinked his eyes open, realizing he'd fallen asleep. He looked at the woman sleeping next to him and realized that they'd figured out a way to build a bridge. They'd talked, made love, and repeated both before they'd both fallen asleep in each other's arms, completely spent. As it was, he was a lucky man but with one big problem. Someone wanted her dead.

Maria's cell buzzed in the other room and he hated waking her. She seemed content and it was the first time she'd looked like that in longer than he could remember.

Denali padded into the room.

"I know, buddy," he said to the dog that moved to his side.

Maria stretched. "How long was I asleep?"

A quick glance at the clock said two hours.

"Was that my phone?" she asked, curling her warm body around him in a way that threatened to get him going again.

He didn't mind but she was probably about to get up and check her cell, so he kissed her and tossed the covers off himself.

"What if we just stay here and let the others handle the case?" she asked, and that would be great if they could.

"I'm all for it." They both seemed to think about Cliff at the same time. "We should probably make sure there isn't news."

Maria yawned before peeling the covers off.

Austin couldn't help himself, he palmed her sweet round bottom as she pushed up and off the bed.

"Do that again and I'm not leaving," she teased, and her voice had that musical quality he loved so much.

Within five minutes they were dressed and she was listening to voice mail. Austin studied her reaction as she listened. Her face paled and then she ended the call.

"Vic is setting up surveillance across the street from a strip shopping center. He's baited a man he believes to be Halpern into a trap. Halpern thinks he's meeting with a thirteen-year-old boy to exchange sexual favors this afternoon. I have to go. I have to see if it's him," she said, and the determination in her eyes spoke volumes about her intent. She needed closure.

"Is it safe for you to be there?" he asked. "I don't want to take unnecessary risks with you. What happened between us changes things for me and I hope like hell it does for you, too."

"If I'm being honest I'm worried that the black cloud that's been following me my entire life will make you miserable," she admitted, and it seemed to take great effort on her part.

"Bad things happen to good people, Maria. No one is immune, not even an O'Brien. You see what we've been through in the past year and you were nowhere near when it happened." He walked over to her and kissed her. "You're not cursed. And just like during a bad storm, you need to know that sunshine always follows. Miserable is living my life without you."

"I've been wanting, no, needing to hear those words for so long, Austin," she said, pushing up on her tiptoes to kiss him back. "But what if I can't give you a family? What if losing Raina means that I'm broken? You'd be sacrificing too much if we couldn't have children."

He shook off her concerns like stray rain droplets. "Family isn't always blood. Look at Tommy. He's no less an O'Brien than I am because he doesn't share the same letters of the alphabet in his last name. If we can't conceive again, then we'll find another way to have a family. Besides, there's no shortage of rug rats running around the ranch lately. If you don't want children we'll be the best damn aunt and uncle an O'Brien has ever seen."

"I love you, Austin," she said, kissing him again.

"Good. Because I love you and I'm not letting you go this time," he said. "Something comes up from now on and we talk it through."

"That's a deal." She beamed up at him and his

heart free-fell. She still had the same effect on him as she did when they first met. She linked their fingers. "I want to make love to my husband again."

He couldn't stop himself from smiling. He picked her up and she wrapped her long legs around his midsection. "What are you waiting for?"

Chapter Seventeen

"The setup is complete," Vic said to her over the phone, and Maria caught on to how tired her boss sounded.

"I want to take a shift on surveillance," she said. "I've spoken to him before and I want to get a sense of his disposition."

"You aren't allowed anywhere near my investigation, remember," Vic said.

"The doc left half an hour ago. The paperwork clearing me to return to work should be in your inbox," she said, thankful that the O'Brien name could move mountains when needed. She'd cashed in a few chips to make that happen.

A moment of silence passed before Vic acquiesced. "You're going to have to fill me in later on how you managed to get the doctor to visit your residence."

That meant he was considering it.

"Can't divulge all my secrets, can I?" she asked, trying to bring levity into the situation. When a dark and tense situation loomed, it was common to make jokes to ease some of the anxiety created by adrenaline. Hers was already starting to pump through her, giving her a jolt of extra energy. Experience had taught her that it would continue until long after the situation went down, leaving her exhausted. It was also the thing that gave her an edge, making her mind sharper and giving a boost to her physical strength. She wanted closure, she wanted Halpern or whoever was responsible for trolling for juveniles to be locked away. And yet, the usual hum of excitement that accompanied the feeling of a case that was about to break open escaped her. She'd always said that when the feeling was gone out of her job that it would be time to walk away. She shelved the thought for now, not sure what to do with it. The only thing she knew for certain was that when this sting was over she planned to talk to her husband about it and listen to his point of view.

After a long pause from Vic, where she figured he was checking his inbox, he finally said, "Fine. You're in."

"Thank you, sir," she said.

"But this is observational only," he warned.

"Got it," she said, thinking she needed to be on guard because Halpern had been great at ambushing her so far. If she got any weird feelings while watching the sting she'd get out of there. "I'll be on my best behavior."

"You'd better be. I need you back on cases ASAP," he demanded, and he was starting to sound like himself.

Instead of confirming, she asked, "How's Cliff?"

"Better. Last night was long but he's sitting up now and asking for fish tacos of all things," he said with a slight chuckle.

"Sounds like him." Relief washed over her at the first sign that maybe no one else would die before this case was solved.

"The nurse gave in but threatened to give him the boot if his wife sneaked in beer," Vic said on another chuckle.

"Then, he'll make a full recovery?" She held her breath until his confirmation came a second later.

Then silence filled the line.

Vic spoke first. "We'll get this dirtbag. I don't care who he turns out to be. He's going down hard for what he's done."

"What makes Wheeler think this might be Halpern?" she asked.

"The accepted invitation came from his IP address," he confirmed.

"That's what I suspected," she stated. "Vic."

"Yeah?" he asked in that nasally voice that said he most likely had a raging headache.

"How many bars are left on the candy?" she asked.

"Three."

"He's going to jail today," she said.

"That's the plan." Vic relayed the details of the sting operation next. Agent Wheeler and Vic would be set up in a mobile command vehicle in the parking lot of a strip shopping center. Another agent would be set up a block behind the center, and in the back of the house where Maria would be. As soon as Halpern showed, he'd be arrested. It sounded simple enough but she had enough experience to know sting operations rarely were executed neatly or went as planned.

Maria jotted down pertinent information of who, when and where.

"I'll keep my head down," she said. "I won't blow our cover."

"I know you won't," he said after a pause.

Austin stood nearby in the kitchen and she could feel his gaze on her. She ended the call with her boss, promising again that no one would recognize her.

"It's going down at four o'clock today," she said. "Vic will be in a mobile unit with Wheeler on the street. There's a house set up for surveillance directly behind the strip mall, which is to be the meet-up point with the undercover 'victim.'"

Austin walked over to her and wrapped his arms around her waist. He looked her in the eyes and asked, "Are you sure this is a good idea?"

"I'm feeling better. My memories have returned. Doc gave me clearance to return to work," she said, and then brought her hands up to his shoulders. "I need to see him arrested. I need to see him locked away. I need that closure so I can move on with my life. As long as he's free I might as well be a prisoner in my own home."

"This is not a bad place to be." Austin eased back a step and folded his arms over his chest. She could tell that she was making headway, which was good because she needed him to be on board.

"Vic said I'm on the sideline for this one. I'm not going to be involved in the arrest," she continued.

"As long as you're not part of the sting," he said. "And as long as I can go with you."

"I'm pretty sure that Vic knows we're a package deal," she said. "Believe me, I'm happy watching from the bench on this one."

He didn't exactly smile but he nodded and that was close enough.

"And when this is over, I want to talk to you about something," she hedged.

"Like what?" he asked.

"Not now. I don't want to jinx anything," she said, trying to lighten the mood. Austin had gotten very serious when she'd called her boss. She couldn't blame him. If the shoe were on the other foot she wouldn't like it, either. Because she was about to come face-to-face with the man who wanted her dead.

MARIA HAD DONNED her Kevlar vest and put on her black FBI hat, keeping it low on her brow in order to shield her face as the officer who'd picked her and Austin up at the field office drove the van through the quiet streets of the suburbs on the east side of Austin.

It was late afternoon in the early days of summer. Watchful mothers kept tabs on kids as they played outside in their yards, taking advantage of the small window of good weather before the blazing Texas sun practically melted the concrete and it was too hot to do anything but splash around in the pool. Even that water would warm at some point, taking away the refreshing feeling of a cold dip. And then it would just be hot.

Vic would be in the mobile command unit with Special Agent Wheeler, who was on tap to make the arrest. He had already touched base with local law enforcement and had an officer assigned to work with him.

If Maria had her preference, she'd be in the mobile command vehicle where the action would be. But she knew better than to push her luck. This was close enough and she was grateful to be included. She wouldn't ask Vic, or Austin for that matter, for more. Besides, if Halpern took one look at her the sting would be busted. There was no way she'd risk the operation.

Adrenaline had her hands trembling as she touched the butt of her gun for reassurance. The grip fit her hand perfectly and there was something comforting about knowing she could protect herself. For Maria, her job had always been about protecting children even when it put her in harm's way.

The operation had been set up quickly and that meant more things could go wrong. Agencies hadn't had a chance to rehearse the sting and that lack of knowledge about how each person liked to operate could end in tragedy if everyone wasn't on constant vigil. The perimeter was unsecure, as well. Maria took everything into account as she prepped her mind. The truth was that stings could and did go wrong. She needed to mentally calculate risk factors in order to provide the best help possible. She could only pray that no one else would be hurt on this assignment.

She'd been paired with a local off-duty cop by the name of Henry Adrienne for the ride over and she'd been told that Special Agent Kendrick waited inside the sting headquarters, which was the house.

Officer Adrienne pulled into the parking garage in the small brick ranch-style home on Pilsner Street.

Maria walked inside first and was greeted by Kendrick. He was on the short side with a stocky build and determined gray eyes.

"Everything's been quiet so far," Kendrick said after introducing himself to Austin.

"I've done my part," Officer Adrienne said. "As much as I'd like to stick around, and believe me when

I say that I would, I've been told my role is over once I successfully hand over 'the package.'"

"Thanks for the ride," Maria said, offering a hand-shake.

Austin, who'd been quiet up until then, offered his thanks as he escorted Adrienne out.

"Is the decoy in place?" Maria asked Kendrick.

"Affirmative," Kendrick said, walking her over to the monitor.

The setup wasn't bad given such short notice. A laptop was connected to a separate 52-inch monitor on top of the breakfast bar. Austin returned and the trio huddled around the screen, which was a live feed of the strip shopping center. Cars eased by on the nearby road. Austin traffic seemed to be at a crawl most of the day and for a second Maria worried Halpern might be stuck somewhere in it.

"How long has he been there?" Maria asked, referring to the kid. He was actually a young under-cover officer posing as a thirteen-year-old boy and looked the part based on his screen image, which had been doctored using a photo-alteration program.

"Ten minutes at the most," Kendrick said after glancing at his watch. He pushed a few buttons on the laptop, raising the volume, and she could hear static from the breeze.

Waiting was the worst.

"How long has the mobile unit been in place?" Maria asked for lack of anything else to say. Austin had been quiet and she knew that he was assessing the situation.

"A couple of hours," Kendrick said. "If he shows and says the right words, we're ready to go."

The snick of a bullet being engaged in a chamber sounded behind them a second before the blast ripped through the air.

All three of them dropped to the floor in a huddle and Maria immediately saw blood splattered on Austin. Kendrick's blood. He'd been shot in the head.

Maria looked up and there stood Halpern, legs wide in an athletic stance. The end of his gun barrel pointed at her. All she could think was that this couldn't be how her life ended.

"I knew you'd be here. All I had to do was follow the marked car. I used to be in the military and am ex–law enforcement and you think I can't spot a setup when I see it? You think I've never worked a case with a doctored photo before?" he asked with a grunt. "I tried to cut you out of the equation before, make your death look like an accident or a random attack but you are persistent."

"What do you want with me?" she asked.

"At first?" His laugh was haughty. "I knew when you didn't recognize me as I passed you outside your building the other day that you'd forgotten who I was. It was only a matter of time before your memories came back after I hit you on the skull. I would've killed you then if I hadn't been interrupted. But the waitress came out for a smoke and I had to take off. You'd figured me out and I have no plans to go to jail."

Austin used his large frame to block her and she took that second to pull her standard-issue weapon. Austin had been banned from bringing his gun, which meant it was her against Halpern and his weapon was already drawn. If she so much as flinched, Halpern would fire and one of them would be dead. Even wearing a bulletproof vest, it was too risky for her to make a move. Austin was in the line of fire and she couldn't allow anything to happen to him.

She prayed like hell that he wouldn't go maverick on her, trying to save her by throwing himself in front of a bullet instead. And that's exactly what someone like him would do.

"The way I see things, this could be a very bad ending for you. It's not too late to get out of this alive," she said to Halpern.

"Oh, but it is for—" he said, and before he could finish his sentence Austin tackled him.

Maria pointed her weapon at Halpern but Austin was in the way as the two tumbled onto the floor. A bullet fired and she immediately called for backup as she watched the two men in a death roll. She couldn't get close enough to see what was really going on without putting Austin in more danger.

Her heart pounded against her ribs and she struggled to breathe against the heavy vest that felt like it was closing in around her. If she moved too close Halpern could use her against Austin. She wouldn't make that mistake. The end of her barrel struggled to find Halpern's body or head, given that he was underneath Austin. *Dammit.* She couldn't get off a clean shot. The twist of bodies rolled toward her and she had to jump back in order to ensure that Halpern couldn't get anywhere near her weapon. She scanned the floor for Halpern's gun but couldn't see it.

Watching the man she loved on the ground fighting for his life was horrific. Maria couldn't imagine worse. She leveled her weapon the second she thought she might be able to get off a clean shot. Austin shifted position, blocking her line of sight. *Dammit. Dammit. Dammit.*

Maria took another step back. And then she saw metal. Halpern's gun was between him and her rancher, and Austin was wrestling for control.

The gun fired. Maria gasped. A bullet whizzed past her head and lodged into the wall behind her.

Maria frantically scanned Austin for signs of a wound. There was no relief because he had blood spatter all over him and she couldn't get a good visual to see if it was from Kendrick—her heart broke for him as he lay on the floor, lifeless—or if Austin had been shot.

"There's no way you're getting out of this, Halpern, even if you do get the best of him. Stop this now. Hand over your weapon and you've got a chance," she said, forcing herself to follow protocol by moving behind the breakfast bar in the open-concept space.

Crouched there, pointing her weapon, she realized how much her hands were shaking. Her legs felt like rubber even though she was on her knees as her worst-case scenario played out in front of her.

Every movement she witnessed sent her stomach soaring like she'd been shot out of an airplane. If there was a chance to help Austin, she would take it. But none was coming and she was getting desperate as she could do nothing more than watch as her husband and Halpern fought for dominance. If she did anything to upset the balance, it could cost Austin his life.

Her heart was in her throat as she helplessly watched as the two of them scrambled around on the floor, kicking and grunting.

Nothing could happen to Austin, dammit. Not after it had taken so long to find their way back to each other.

"Surrender your weapon, Halpern. We know who you are. There's nowhere to go that we won't find you. I'm your way out of this. I'm your only choice." She used a louder, urgent, high-pitched tone this time. Halpern would recognize the law enforcement tactic meant to catch him off guard.

There was no response, only more grunting and more struggle. And more of her heartbeat hammering her throat. She heard the back door open and Vic ask for clearance.

"Make them go away," Halpern managed to grunt.

"Can you move out?" Vic asked.

"Negative, sir. I won't leave," she said. "We have an agent down and a man in trouble. I'm taking the first clear shot I see." She said that last part especially loudly for Halpern's benefit. He wasn't going to stop until either he or Austin couldn't get up. As it was, Austin had a chance. But if Halpern believed that he was going to kill the man she loved and walk away he was sadly mistaken. Halpern was either going to jail or to the grave today. She had no plans to let him slip through her fingers this time. And especially not if he got the best of Austin.

In the next second, Austin rolled on top of Halpern. Both of his hands gripped Halpern's. Another bullet split the air, veering left. Austin looked to have Halpern somewhat under control.

Maria was on her feet, crouched low, ready to seize if the right opportunity presented itself.

A moment later, Austin had control of the gun. His knees were a viselike grip around Halpern's torso and arms. The weapon was pointed at his forehead.

"Go ahead and shoot," Halpern said with a sneer, trying to wiggle away.

Maria called for reinforcement. FBI flooded the place. And before she could process what had just happened—her freedom—Halpern was facedown and being zip-cuffed.

Austin rolled onto his back, panting, and she rushed to his side as other agents attended to Kendrick. She said a silent prayer for the slain agent and her heart grieved for the loss.

An hour later, statements had been given and they'd both cleaned up and been given fresh shirts.

It was over. Tears streamed down Maria's face as she repeated those words over and over again.

"I'm done here. Take me home," she said to her husband.

A GOOD NIGHT of sleep gave Maria much-needed reprieve. She woke thinking it was time to gain a new perspective. There'd been so much loss. It was time to focus forward and create a new life. She stretched, missing the feel of Austin's warm body.

Noises came from the kitchen and she could hear her husband talking to the dogs. The smell of fresh coffee convinced her to get out of bed.

She washed her face and brushed her teeth before joining him. He smiled at her and kissed her. And she couldn't think of a better way to start each day.

"Got a call from Dallas," he said.

"What happened with Bea and Ezra?" she asked, taking the mug he offered.

"They're going to jail for the rest of their lives. Bea confessed that everything had been her idea. Turns out she'd been the one trying to cut a deal with McCabe and she thought she'd get access to the back acreage if she threw in her share of the ranch to entice us."

"McCabe must've been offering a lot of money," she said, taking a sip.

"He had a lot to burn before being sent to prison,"

he agreed. "She thought it was all over after his arrest but Tommy was getting too close to figuring out the truth so she tried to erase evidence."

"And that's what she was doing at the house the other day when Denali almost got her busted." Maria shook her head, thinking that greed rarely got people what they truly wanted. "And Ezra was set up to look suspicious all this time because he'd have an ironclad alibi…her."

Austin nodded, those intense green eyes on her.

"We decided their shares of the ranch will go to Tommy. He's more like family than our aunt and uncle ever could be."

Maria set down her cup and threw her arms around Austin's neck. "That's one of the many things I love about this family. You really are the good guys."

Austin looped his arms around her. "I'm having some unholy thoughts right now."

She laughed.

"Not so fast, Ivy League. We need to talk first," she said.

"That's a mood killer," he teased. And she could tell he was joking by the sparkle in his eyes. After all they'd been through, they needed humor.

"I'm done with the Bureau," Maria said to her husband.

"But I thought you loved your job." Austin didn't seem able to hide his shock.

"I loved the idea of helping kids, *really* helping

them. Locking someone away and making them pay for what they did was…satisfying on some level. But no matter how many bad guys I put behind bars, I couldn't quiet my own demons," she said.

"Are you sure that will help? I'm all for you quitting for the right reasons. Don't do this for me," he warned. "Because I love you no matter what line of work you're in and above all I want you to be happy."

"There are so many ways to help children that don't involve a gun," she said. "The way it is now I lock the bad guy away and say that I've done my job but what happens to the kids next? They've been traumatized by someone and then what? Everything's supposed to be okay just because the person who hurt them is behind bars? That's temporary, you know? They have to face getting through the ordeal and that's where we fall short. I'd rather become a counselor and work with them when everyone disappears and the dust settles, when they're supposed to pick up with their lives and move on. Only they can't possibly know how."

She looked at him, his bold green eyes examining her.

"I think I know what you mean." He kissed her. "You want to be there to help them put the pieces of their lives back together."

"Exactly. I wish there would've been someone around to help me do that," she said.

"What about Vic?" Austin rubbed the scruff on his chin. "He'll be devastated if you leave."

Maria laughed. She wouldn't deny that statement was partly true. "I'll give him plenty of time to replace me. There's no shortage of good people willing and able to do my job."

"You're sure about all this?" Austin asked. There was more hope in his eyes than he'd ever admit.

She ran her finger lazily along his muscled arm. "I wouldn't be walking away *just* to be a fancy farmer's wife."

He started to protest her use of the word *farmer*. She stopped him.

"Before you get all crazy detailing out the difference between a farmer and a rancher, I'd like to say something else," she said.

He smirked.

"I might be walking away from something, but I'll be walking *toward* a job that will mean more to me than everything but the man I love, my husband. *You*," she said, like he needed clarification.

That really did elicit a smile from her Texas rancher.

"I'll be walking *toward* a job that I want to do rather than need to hide inside," she added.

His smile broadened, revealing his perfect white teeth.

"And I'll be walking *toward* a project that I've been wanting to talk to you about," she said, searching his gaze.

"You already know I'll go along with whatever

you want. All you have to do is ask," he said, his grip tightening around her waist.

"I was hoping you'd say that because what I want is…a big deal," she said.

"Are you planning to tell me or keep me in suspense all day," he teased.

"A baby."

Fear seized her when he didn't immediately respond. Was this too much, too soon?

He picked her up and walked her straight to the bedroom without saying a word. Before she could ask what he was thinking, he was on top of her, balancing most of his weight on muscled arms and strong knees. He dipped down to kiss her before locking onto her gaze.

"That project might take a little time, so I think it'd be best if we started working on it right now," he said with the sexiest little smile.

Maria pulled him down on top of her, loving the feel of his weight on her and how it pressed her back into the mattress. "I can't think of a better time to start than now."

He kissed her so hard it robbed her of breath. All she could think was that she'd finally found it…the place that she truly belonged…she'd found home.

* * * * *

SPECIAL EXCERPT FROM

mira

*Special agent Griffin Price and historian Vickie Preston
are on their way to start a new life together. But a romantic
weekend detour is interrupted when a popular author
is found dead under mysterious circumstances in the
basement of a local restaurant, and the FBI's Krewe of
Hunters paranormal team is brought in to investigate...*

Read on for a sneak preview of
WICKED DEEDS,
the next installment in the **KREWE OF HUNTERS** *series*
from New York Times *bestselling author*
Heather Graham.

Vickie reached out and set her hand over Monica's. "I'm so sorry."

Monica Verne looked at Vickie and nodded. Griffin thought that Vickie's ability to feel with others and offer them real comfort was going to be one of her greatest assets in joining the Krewe. It was also going to be one of the most difficult parts of the job for her to learn to manage. He lowered his head for a moment; it was an odd time to smile. And an odd time to think just how lucky he was. Vickie was beautiful to look at—five foot eight, with long raven black waves of hair and blue-green eyes that could change and shimmer like emeralds.

She was also so caring—honest and filled with integrity.

He truly loved her. Watching her empathy and gentle touch with Monica, he knew all the more reason why.

"My husband didn't kill himself!" Monica whispered fervently.

"I don't think it's been suggested that he killed himself.

I believe they're considering it an accidental death," Griffin began.

"Accidental death, my ass! If there's any last thing I can do for Franklin, it's going to be to make someone prove that this was no accidental death!" Monica lashed out, indignant. She wasn't angry with Vickie—who was still holding her hand. Her passion was against the very suggestion that her husband's death had been through a simple slip—some misfortune.

She wagged a finger at Griffin. "You listen to me, and listen well. We were the best, Frankie and me. I swear it. When all else fell to hell and ruin, we still had one another… Franklin did not meet up with a friend! He did not break into that cellar to drink himself to death! I'm telling you, I knew my husband, he…"

She broke off, gritting her teeth. She was trying not to cry. The woman was truly in anguish; she was also furious.

"I don't know when he went out. I don't know why he went out—or how he wound up at the restaurant. I do know one thing."

"What is that, Mrs. Verne?" Vickie asked.

Monica Verne startled them both, slamming a fist on the coffee table. "My husband was murdered!"

The motion seemed to be a cue.

In the yard, a dozen birds took flight, shrieking and cawing.

Griffin could see them as they let out their cries, sweeping into the sky.

A murder of crows…

And an unkindness of ravens…

As poetically cruel as the death of Franklin Verne.

WICKED DEEDS
by New York Times *bestselling author Heather Graham.*
Available now from MIRA® Books.

www.Harlequin.com

MHGEXP1017

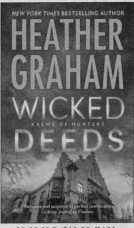

NEW YORK TIMES BESTSELLING AUTHOR

HEATHER GRAHAM

WICKED

KREWE OF HUNTERS

DEEDS

Romance and suspense in perfect combination.
—*Library Journal* on *Flawless*

$8.99 U.S./$10.99 CAN.

$1.00 OFF

New York Times bestselling author

HEATHER GRAHAM

returns with the next
action-packed romantic suspense story
in the *Krewe of Hunters* series.

WICKED DEEDS

Available now.

mira

Harlequin.com

$1.00 OFF the purchase price of WICKED DEEDS by Heather Graham.

Offer valid from September 19, 2017, to October 31, 2017.
Redeemable at participating retail outlets, in-store only. Not redeemable at
Barnes & Noble. Limit one coupon per purchase. Valid in the U.S.A. and Canada only.

52615115

5 65373 00076 2 (8100)0 12306

Canadian Retailers: Harlequin Enterprises Limited will pay the face value of this coupon plus 10.25¢ if submitted by customer for this product only. Any other use constitutes fraud. Coupon is nonassignable. Void if taxed, prohibited or restricted by law. Consumer must pay any government taxes. Void if copied. Inmar Promotional Services ("IPS") customers submit coupons and proof of sales to Harlequin Enterprises Limited, PO Box 31000, Scarborough, ON M1R 0E7, Canada. Non-IPS retailer—for reimbursement submit coupons and proof of sales directly to Harlequin Enterprises Limited, Retail Marketing Department, 225 Duncan Mill Rd., Don Mills, ON M3B 3K9, Canada.

U.S. Retailers: Harlequin Enterprises Limited will pay the face value of this coupon plus 8¢ if submitted by customer for this product only. Any other use constitutes fraud. Coupon is nonassignable. Void if taxed, prohibited or restricted by law. Consumer must pay any government taxes. Void if copied. For reimbursement submit coupons and proof of sales directly to Harlequin Enterprises, Ltd 482, NCH Marketing Services, P.O. Box 880001, El Paso, TX 88588-0001, U.S.A. Cash value 1/100 cents.

® and ™ are trademarks owned and used by the trademark owner and/or its licensee.

© 2017 Harlequin Enterprises Limited

MCOUPHG1017

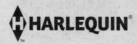